To Margaret,

Thank you for traveling with Esperanza.

LF Escandón

ESPERANZA'S
Box of Saints

María Amparo Escandón

SCRIBNER PAPERBACK FICTION
Published by Simon & Schuster

SCRIBNER PAPERBACK FICTION
Simon & Schuster Inc.
Rockefeller Center
1230 Avenue of the Americas
New York, NY 10020

Designed by Brooke Zimmer
Illustrations by Christian Clayton
Set in Dante MT
Manufactured in the United States of America

1 3 5 7 9 10 8 6 4 2

Library of Congress Cataloging-in-Publication Data
Escandón, María Amparo.
Esperanza's box of saints / María Amparo Escandón.
p.   cm.
I. Mexican Americans—Fiction. I. Title.
PS3555.S264E85   1999
813'.54—dc21   98-29552
CIP

ISBN 0-684-85614-X

To San Judas Tadeo for the miracle granted.
And to Benito, Marinés, and Iñaki,
because they are the miracle.

Which pain is so unequal in its effect,
that being of sorrows the most profound,
heals a deeper grief?

—*Sor Juana Inés de la Cruz, Enigma # 3*

ESPERANZA'S
Box of Saints

"It's me again, Father Salvador, Esperanza Díaz, the mother of the dead girl. Only she's not dead. I should have told you the last time I came for confession. But I didn't dare. The words just turned their backs on me, like disloyal friends.

"I've come every day. I stand by the altar waiting for you to finish Mass. Then I go home. I've been thinking all week, if someone is to hear what's happened, it's you. It's not that I have a sin to confess. Well, I do, a little one, but I'll save it for later. What I really came for is to confide to you something the Church should know. I can't tell anyone else. No one would believe me. You see, I witnessed an apparition.

"The night of the funeral I prayed to San Judas Tadeo, our saint for desperate cases. You know how miraculous he is. Why is he so good to me? I guess that's why he's a saint and I'm not. It takes a good-hearted kind of person to become a saint. He's been among my favorite ones ever since I was a little girl. There's a special place for him in our church. Often as a little girl I'd sneak in just to chat with him and stare at the medallion shining on his chest. It's so big, Father, and the saint is so small. At least the one by the side of the altar, to the right of the Virgen de la Candelaria, our patron saint of Tlacotalpan. He must be doing some major sacrifice by carrying all that weight forever and ever around his neck. I even climbed up the pedestal once to check if the medallion was hollow. It wasn't. Solid gold is what he's been carrying all this time. And I don't see why not. His cousin Jesus couldn't have had a better saint to entrust all that wealth to. But that is not what I admire most in him. It's his supernatural ability to watch over so many people in desperate situations at once. Well, what can we expect? He has been blessed with all the heavenly powers within and beyond our imagination. He is way up there in God's hierarchy. Not everyone is willing to be killed with stones for spreading our Lord's word.

"And then, what happens to me, of all people? A week ago his image appeared before me, on my oven window. I was baking pollo al chipotle for the funeral guests. I can never get that sauce right. I don't even want to tell you what that kitchen looked like when I was done. I put too much cream in the blender and it spilled over to the counter. I forgot to put onions in the chicken broth and it tasted like water used to soak soiled socks. I put in more salt than I was supposed to. I didn't take the seeds out of the peppers. I greased the Pyrex and shouldn't have. I would have been embarrassed if my mother had seen me. But ever since she passed away, may she rest in peace, I haven't had that feeling of embarrassment. She took it with her, I guess.

"People were coming over at seven o'clock to offer me their condolences. And to check out the kitchen. They can't help but notice if you're tidy or not so they can talk behind your back. This time I didn't disappoint them. I was just too sad to clean up the mess. It's not every day that my only daughter is buried.

"I hadn't cleaned the oven in months. And now I realize it hasn't been procrastination. A heavenly reason was causing my untidiness. San Judas Tadeo needed the grime to appear to me. I looked at the glass at an angle so as not to confuse the reflection of my face with his image. I saw his green velvet robe and his sparkling gold medallion. The image came and went until it settled on the murky glass, like when the moon, sort of insecure, reflects itself on the Papaloapan River.

"Suddenly, all the noises in the street stopped. I couldn't hear them coming through the open window. The children's screams when they play jacks on the sidewalk, the whistle of the one-eyed man who sharpens knives, the church bells' chime announcing bedtime, the street dogs' howls looking for their mates. All gone. The ticktock of the clock on my living room wall stopped, too, although I checked later and it had kept on going throughout the entire apparition. The pungent smells of chili in the kitchen became almost sweet, like fresh-cut gardenias.

"I sat on the floor. I couldn't feel its coldness. I didn't care. I looked real hard at the oven window, and there he was. He wasn't flat like a painting. He had depth. Weight. He floated toward me, like a piñata dangling from a rope. The grease drippings shone like amber. He looked directly into my eyes. He was so beautiful. His hair was blond and a little curly. He had a beard, just like Jesus Christ. He said, 'Your daughter is not dead . . .' I said, 'San Judas, San Judas.' I thought he was going to continue and I tried to touch him, but then the image disappeared and I burned my finger. I'd show you the blister, but I just covered it with a clean Band-Aid before coming.

"I wonder why apparitions are always so brief. Why do saints come down to the world of the living, give us a couple of signs, and leave in a hurry? Why don't they stay a bit longer? Is it because Heaven is so marvelous that they don't want to leave even for just a few seconds? Perhaps earth is just too sad a place for them. Are they afraid they might lose their spot by our Lord's side if they get up to visit us? So you see, I was left with more questions than answers. I wanted to ask San Judas Tadeo why God had taken Blanca from me so early in her life. And if she isn't dead, where is she? That's when I figured that the doctor at the hospital had lied when he said she was killed by a very contagious disease that doesn't yet have a name.

"After the apparition I asked myself, 'Should I clean the oven, or should I leave it as it is?' I guess for now I won't touch it. After all, that's where my saint decided to appear. If he likes it there, I respect his preferences. And maybe he'll come back to explain what he said. So the oven is going to stay dirty. It's a problem to get rid of grease stains, Father. Well, how could you know, now that I think about it? You have Doña Carmelita to take care of you. I know she cooks for you every day and does your laundry. I've seen her come to your home in the morning and leave in the afternoon. And before her someone at the seminary took care of you, I suppose. And before that no doubt you had your mother and an army of sisters. In any case, I'm sure you're at least a bit familiar with grime. And I don't mean the grime in our souls. I mean the kind that builds up on a regular oven.

"My *comadre* Soledad found me on the floor crying and helped me to the living room couch. For some reason I expected her to look different after the miracle I had just experienced. I don't know, a glow around her head, a sign that we had all become pure and virtuous after San Judas Tadeo's visit. But, really, Father Salvador, she was the same Soledad I had known since we sat side by side on our little first-grade bench. Her same stark eyes, black and small and lost under layers of loneliness. Her chubby cheeks, probably stolen from a careless angel sometime during her childhood. Her arms, broad and sturdy like a magnolia's trunk, ending with scrawny, delicate fingers, twigs, disproportionate to the rest of her hefty figure. She has saved her tears for when I'm not around. I know she has cried, she cries a lot, but I haven't been there when she does it. All she did was embrace me and pretend to be the strong one. The one whose shoulder I should lean on for the next fifty years.

"Two hours later, I had to sit and kiss and hug people who I knew would go about their normal lives again as soon as they left my house. A parent meeting was being held at school the following night. They were talking about that. I'm in charge of publicity for the carnival coming up. I made the posters myself and put them up on the ice cream shop's refrigerator door, at the hospital's front desk, and on the church's bulletin board. I was supposed to get a new assignment at the next meeting, only now I have no daughter enrolled in the school. I won't have to go to meetings anymore.

"But I haven't told you the details. With the rush to bury her and the funeral arrangements and the Mass, I haven't really sat down with you to talk about all this. Blanca died the day she was to be discharged from the hospital. She had her tonsils out. I had them out when I was twelve, too. I thought we could start a family tradition. When she was in the operating room and I waited outside, I imagined, many years from now, Blanca's own daughter having her tonsils out as soon as she turned twelve. It could have been one of those things families do one generation after another without questioning why. Every member of the Díaz family must go through the same kind of surgery at the age of twelve. It could have been perpetuated forever. But my family stopped with Blanca. All that's left of this tradition are her tonsils floating in a jar filled with formaldehyde sitting on my coffee table. And my own surgery, of course. I think about it often. Maybe it's the very reason why my words get stuck in my throat during difficult moments. I must have a big scar.

"So anyway, Father, I don't want to keep you much longer. There are four people behind me who are waiting for confession. I just have one little sin: I bad-mouthed my *comadre* Soledad. On the bus to Alvarado two weeks before Blanca disappeared, I met a woman from Veracruz and we talked about ourselves as if we were best friends. Perhaps precisely because we were not, my feelings about Soledad surfaced more easily. I would not see that woman again. Different towns. Different lives. She is an assistant branch manager at a bank. I don't even have an account. I thought it was safe to tell her about Soledad. The gossip would not make it to her ears. And now I feel remorse. But it's not fair, Father. I come home every night after working a full shift and keeping the accounting books up to date at the hardware store. Yet I am the one who has to iron all our clothes. All she does is sit around and make Jarocha costumes for weddings, parades, and pilgrimages. You know she's the best dressmaker in town, but that is no excuse for her lack of tidiness. And if this weren't enough, she has the television on all day and watches the soap operas, as if we didn't have enough tragedy in our lives. If she lives with me, she should at least pick up after herself. She won't even make her own bed. I know she keeps me company and I appreciate it, but I'm getting tired of dealing with her mess. And that's not the only thing that annoys me. She complains about her health all day. She develops a backache right before we need to lift a crate of oranges. She suffers from menstrual cramps even when she doesn't have her period. Sometimes her hair hurts. Her blood aches. Her fingernails become sore. But she won't go to the doctor. Now, you see? Here I am, bad-mouthing her again.

"It's been like this for twelve years now. And I haven't even tried talking to her. How can you change the personality of a thirty-five-year-old woman? I know there's more to it than just bad-mouthing her. My sin is really bigger than it looks. Because I do care for her. I've known her since we were little girls, but at times I wish she was the one who disappeared. Not my Blanca. But whether I like it or not, I don't see myself living without Soledad. We're meant to share the rest of our lives with each other. When both our husbands hurled down the Cumbres de Acultzingo ravine in that bus twelve years ago, may they rest in peace, God decided that Soledad and I should raise my daughter Blanca together.

"Remember that accident, Father? Maybe you hadn't been transferred to Tlacotalpan yet. It was famous. Everyone was killed, including five people from our town. When they finally located the wreckage at the bottom of the ravine, after the bus had fallen headlong through the clouds trapped between those endless walls covered with ferns, the first to be recovered were our two husbands. Their bodies were found lying on the ground, completely splattered with eight brilliant colors. That's the main reason I could tell the corpse was Luis' when I went to identify him at the morgue. Colonial blue on his left shoulder. Parakeet yellow across his face. Orchid magenta down his pants. Avocado green messing up his hair. Geranium pink on his upper back.

Pansy purple covering a shoe. Sunset orange staining his shirt. Poinsettia red blending with blood from a cut on his neck. Oh, God. Every single can of paint they were bringing as samples to the distributor in Orizaba was open and lying empty around their bodies. I picture Luis and Alfredo chatting, just before the bus hit the donkey in the middle of the road. As the bus turned over, they must have tried to hold on to their seats, leaving the paint's destination to gravity.

"While our husbands were away on business trips, selling paint from town to town, Soledad stayed at my house so that we could keep each other company. The four of us were very close. Oftentimes we traveled together. Once we went to the ancient ruins of Tajín. Alfredo borrowed a car from his brother-in-law. He let Alfredo take it because he knew he was a very good driver. Alfredo showed off his ability making the car skid and setting it back on course by just steering the wheel with one finger. Luis yelled at him all the time. Soledad hyperventilated. She never sat in the passenger seat. She rode in the back with me. I've always wondered how upset Alfredo must have been as he was falling into the precipice the day he was killed, being such a skilled driver and dying at the hands of a bad bus driver. Destiny has twisted ways of reminding us we don't own our future.

"But most of the times Soledad and I didn't travel with our husbands. On the fatal trip, Soledad stayed to help me with my newborn baby, my Blanca. Soledad is her godmother, you know? When we became widows, she left the house she rented and moved in with me. You see how God reworks events so that our path gets more and more entangled and we end up having relationships that seem at first as if they were not meant to be? I've been trying to learn how to live with her ever since.

"That's the sin, Father Salvador. But I can carry it longer if I need to. What I really want is to find Blanca, now that San Judas Tadeo has told me she is not dead. So, I must be going. Please come up with my penance. I promise I'll be back soon. And I'll keep an eye on the oven window. In the name of the Father and of the Son and of the Holy Ghost. Amen."

Dear God, did You hear that woman's confession this afternoon? Did You get the whole thing about the apparition? Oh, please, help me on this one. In my thirty-two years as a priest, I have never heard firsthand of an individual witnessing one. There was the time when San Juan Nepomuceno appeared on the bridge wall five years ago. Everyone in town saw his image forming in the moss. The pilgrimages to the site went on until the summer when the river grew with the rains and covered the bridge. The water took every altar and offering all the way to the ocean. Plastic flowers, wreaths, ex-votos, photographs of children showing their brand-new teeth, a thick black braid tied with a pink bow. Some people claim they've seen novena candles still lit, floating on the waves at night like tiny boats, up and down, up and down, thousands of kilometers away.

That really was a collective miracle. But this is different. Why is San Judas Tadeo appearing to Mrs. Díaz in such a private way? Is she telling the truth? What do his words mean? I told her to keep the apparition to herself. I didn't know what else to say. I wanted to consult with You before giving her more advice. This is not an easy story to believe. People may think she's just overwhelmed by her daughter's death. And it might be precisely that. As You see, this is a very delicate matter. I must guide her through this so she finds her daughter, or comes to terms with her death. So please, dear God, help me. And now, I have to go. It's almost eight o'clock and I don't want to miss my soap opera. Tonight, Elizabeth-Constanza finds out she has a blind twin sister. Amen.

"I'm glad our wives didn't come with us."

"Well, Luis, they almost talked us into it. Esperanza is so determined."

"I can imagine her bringing the baby and a truckload of diapers and toys and gadgets. This is a business trip. She's better off at home."

"Don't worry. Soledad can help her. She has always helped watch my sister's babies."

"But Blanquita is special. She cries so much when she's not in my arms."

"They'll be fine without us. We're only going away for a week. Did you pack all the paint samples?"

"Eight. We're presenting eight colors to the distributor, right?"

"But are you sure we're not bringing two samples of the same color? Let's open the cans and check. Just to make sure."

"When are you gonna let me rest?"

Esperanza walked through town toward her house. The house had stood for over two hundred years silently witnessing the lives of her family's generations. Many layers of paint covered it. These days bright egg yolk yellow bounced off the walls. Bougainvillea pink lines ran along the borders of every opening, embracing the old door and covering the bottom half wall. Cobalt blue wrought-iron posts guarded the windows, anticipating the very unlikely possibility of a break-in.

Luis had picked those colors before he was killed in the bus accident. Esperanza had it painted the way he wanted and kept it like that for more than twelve years, missing him more every day, reading his letters over and over and saving them in a tin marzipan candy box under her bed, along with newspaper clippings from the accident, his wedding ring, his wisdom tooth, a few strands of his hair—stiff and glued together with a dry blotch of green paint—and a key chain with their photo, his arm around her, taken when they went to visit the Virgen de Guadalupe in Mexico City.

A reasonable, prudent time after Luis' death, six men came forward all at once and claimed to love Esperanza. They wished they could caress her long black hair and hold her close for at least one century.

The first one hoped to marry her and give her three boys so she could be safe and taken care of in her old age. The boys would become doctors, lawyers, or engineers, if that's what it took to make her love him.

The second man's desire was to build her a modern house with air-conditioning and paint it with the colors she liked best and then make love to her in every one of the rooms, every day of the week at different hours of the day, so sunlight could reflect on the colored walls and bounce back on their skins, making them blue, then green, then orange.

The third man belonged to the wealthiest family in town. He owned a sugar cane factory and swore he would make Esperanza's life as sweet as he hoped her lips to be. He admired the way she sometimes held them open a tiny bit in a hint of a smile, revealing her straight, resplendent white teeth.

The fourth man, a Mexico City native, threatened to

kill himself if Esperanza didn't pay attention to him. He followed her to church every Sunday for eight months, attracted mainly by the way her hips swayed like a boat when she walked.

The fifth man wanted to feel her large, firm breasts pressed against his chest and was known to sleep every night holding a pillow as if it were Esperanza. He made the mistake of telling this to his barber, who in turn told the rest of his clients, sending the gossip all the way to the neighboring town of Alvarado. Often he would be asked at social gatherings, "And how's Mrs. Pillow?"

The sixth man, a sailor, wanted to take her on a trip around the world. His plan was to stop at every island and make love on the shore, where curious seagulls could glance at them and die of envy after realizing what they missed for not being human.

But in the end, except for the fourth man, who was ultimately locked up in a mental hospital, they all had to marry other women, so tired had they become of waiting for Esperanza to even greet them on the street.

"I couldn't love any of those men," she told Soledad once while walking home from the market. "God gave me my chance with Luis. Too bad it didn't last long. I'll just be a widow and that's that."

Luis fell in love with Esperanza at eight-fifteen in the morning on the first day of tenth grade when she walked into the classroom. He couldn't help but notice her hair, long and a bit wavy, like the river water on a windy afternoon. And just looking at it hanging loosely down her shoulders and over her back made him light-headed. He saw her scan the room in search of an empty desk, greet the teacher, and sit down in the third row. Another empty desk was next to him. Hadn't she seen it? Why was she sitting so far away? Had she caught him staring at her? Had she seen him break out in a sweat the minute she walked in? Could she have noticed the pimple on his nose? Maybe she didn't want to sit next to him, the new kid in the classroom.

Luis had been unabashedly happy since preschool, but on that day, he silently admitted to himself that he had wasted sixteen years of his life, which meant all of it. Why had God sent him to earth so long before he saw that girl? He thought of the millions of minutes wasted with his friends at the Alvarado wharf talking about girls they'd like to go to bed with, walking younger girls home from school and imagining them naked, posting magazine cutouts of teen beauties behind his closet door and masturbating on mosquito-infested nights. Suddenly, every woman he knew became small, insignificant, a midget next to the girl who sat in the third row.

Esperanza didn't notice Luis until recess, at ten-thirty. He sat at the far end of the schoolyard, protected by the shade of a generous mango tree. The heat was oppressive. The sun was cruel. He drank a tamarind soda straight from the bottle and offered Esperanza a sip with a wordless gesture that she understood clear across the yard. And since she just had to get a closer look at his smile, she walked over and sat by him until the bell rang, fifteen minutes later. They exchanged names. They laughed for no particular reason. They shared the tamarind soda. By day's end, they had already written each other notes that went from hand to hand across the classroom.

He wrote: "Life has been senseless until today. Let's make up for the time we haven't been together."

She answered: "Come for dinner with my parents at eight o'clock."

From that evening until years later when Luis was killed in the bus accident, Esperanza felt that each hour they spent together was worth three. They loved each other with hurried passion. Their kisses did not have the taste of eternity. It was during those days that Esperanza's skin began developing a tamarind-candy flavor. Bitter, sweet, sour, and salty, all at the same time. Her flesh was like a planet with one harmonious nation. A luscious fruition for Luis' taste buds. A sacred shrine for mosquitoes. A potential threat to those with weak stomachs. Every night, he spent one hour licking her, starting behind her ear and ending between her toes.

After his death, his pictures, framed in wood, silver, pewter, plastic, and bamboo, hung from the walls, stood on the bookshelf, on the kitchen table, by her bed, and at the door. Every day, Esperanza spent a few seconds looking at each one and wondering how she would get by in his absence. She kept herself busy making sure the accounting books were up to date at the hardware store, helping Soledad iron the Jarocha costumes she designed, and visiting her parents and Luis at the cemetery.

And then there was little Blanca to care for. She was born a very small baby, two months before her due date, perhaps because she knew, in her mother's womb, that if she didn't hurry, she would never be held in her father's arms. And in fact, during her first four weeks of life, it was mainly Luis who held her. If anyone else picked her up from her crib, she'd cry tears the size of an adult's. Esperanza came to think her baby didn't love her, but Blanca was just getting the most attention she could from a father she would not have for long. As soon as Luis died, Blanca's crying stopped and Esperanza's began.

The door of Esperanza's house was stubborn at times and refused to open. But she found a way to jiggle her key in the old lock until it gave in. She amused herself thinking she tickled it with the key and that the squeaking sound the door made when it opened was its laughter.

"Where were you?" Soledad was waiting for Esperanza on the patio. She sounded concerned. A habit of hers. "The Espinozas came by to express their condolences."

"I went to see Father Salvador. I told him all about Blanca."

Esperanza whimpered on Soledad's shoulder, tired of crying so much those past few days. Soledad squeezed a couple of little tears out. They seemed petty, almost inadequate, but to Esperanza those tears meant that her friend was finally allowing herself to be vulnerable.

"I shouldn't be crying in front of you," said Soledad.

"It's fine. You don't always have to be strong."

They exchanged handkerchiefs and dried each other's tears.

"You're as hard as an oak tree, Soledad. Can't you just break down once for me?"

"I am breaking down." Soledad wiped a single tear off her cheek and smeared it on Esperanza's palm. "See?"

Esperanza knew Soledad cried inconsolably at certain moments during her beloved soap operas, yet when it came to her own tragedies, she would always act as if she could take anything. At her husband's funeral, she was the only one who did not cry, at least in public. Because of that, many people believed that Soledad had never really loved Alfredo, that she had married him just because he resembled the late Mexican movie idol Pedro Infante. This gossip went on for a few years, until one day, while ordering a birthday cake for Blanca at the bakery, Esperanza overheard two women talking about the issue. She took two meringue cupcakes topped with whipped cream from the counter, paid for them, and once given the change, smashed them on the women's heads. From then on, the gossip focused on Esperanza's temper. And it didn't stop until Esperanza tied a coin to the mouth of San Ramón Nonato, always called on for protection against people talking behind one's back. She fastened the coin to the saint's statue with a red ribbon, passing the ribbon around his head and making three knots at the back of his neck.

Soledad and Esperanza tiptoed across the patio, so as not to wake her grandfather's hydrangea sleeping in terra-cotta pots and old motor fuel oil cans. Hundreds of containers—tin, plastic, majolica, wood, cement—were carefully arranged in groups all over the brick floor and around the magnolia tree. The women knew well where to set their feet as they walked in the semidarkness toward the door at the end of the cluttered patio.

As they settled themselves in the living room, a major drama involving two angry, handsome men developed before their eyes on the TV set, but they did not pay attention.

"What are we going to do with so much pain?" Soledad's voice was brittle. "If it keeps growing it won't fit in our bodies anymore."

"The worst part is that we're crying for no reason." Esperanza was blunt. "Blanca is not dead."

This was the first of many times when Soledad would question Esperanza's mental health. To her, the girl's death was a fact as clear and tangible as the funeral itself. She had signed the death certificate as a witness, she had seen the casket being covered with dirt at the cemetery, and she had prayed for Blanca's soul along with the sixty or so other people who attended the service. Clearly, the next step was to mourn her, accept the fact with resignation, and move on.

"San Judas Tadeo told me." Esperanza bit her lip. "In person." She bit it again. How could she be saying this? She had promised Father Salvador to keep the miracle to herself.

"For God's sake, Esperanza. Don't go crazy on me."

Their conversation became tangled with the one coming from the soap opera on TV, a braid of words overlapping one another, trying to make sense.

"I never thought that my own partner would backstab me this way. Those signed checks were blank and you knew it. You're a fortune thief, Carlos Alberto! A thief of hearts!" said one of the well-groomed men on the TV screen.

"You don't believe me." Esperanza realized then why Father Salvador had asked her to keep the apparition a secret.

"She set the amount on those checks! Forget about your daughter, José Fernando, she's mine from now on, body, soul, and bank accounts!" A younger man, more handsome, his mustache a bit uneven, yelled in a close-up almost too big for the screen.

Esperanza didn't wait for the other man to answer. She stood up, turned the TV off, and walked away from Soledad.

"I just want everything to be the way it was before we lost Blanca," she said at the door, leaving Soledad alone in the living room.

A very large living room, it seemed to Soledad. The whole house had suddenly become a big empty place. The kitchen, the bedrooms, the dining room, all were now filled with heat and nothingness. Sunlight refused to come in through the windows. The hallway was silent, devoid of Blanca's laughter. Chairs and armoires and tables had lost their purpose. She felt she didn't belong in Esperanza's house anymore. With the girl gone, she no longer had a reason to live there. Blanca didn't need her. Souls that live with God don't need little dressmaking godmothers. But if Esperanza was losing her mind, she would have to stay and take care of her.

Soledad dragged the rocking chair to the portico and sat, staring at the street as if something interesting might happen. She, too, wanted everything to be the way it had been when Blanca was around. Just a few months before, she had begun making her a Jarocha costume. In her lifetime she had made dozens of those elaborate dresses for the most beautiful girls and women in Tlacotalpan to wear at their Quince Años dances and Candelaria festivities. But her goddaughter's dress had to be special. Far more embroidery would be involved. Imported satin. First-class organza. Esperanza's slip, worn also by her mother and her grandmother. The shoes, brought in from the city. During the last fitting, a couple of weeks before Blanca died, Soledad enveloped her tender preteen body with the white fabric, making her look like a child angel surrounded by voluptuous clouds. She remembered Blanca in the dress, halfway made, pins sticking out everywhere, wearing a tiny bra that bashfully covered breasts the size of mosquito bites. Even at that ungraceful age, not yet a woman, and no longer a girl, Blanca was pretty. Her body was beginning to swell in the places men crave the most. Her hair, long and black, like the wings of a magpie, fell over her bare shoulders. This was a girl who would not suffer from acne, would not need braces, would not gain weight, would not smoke or follow teenage fads, and still, one whom all her friends at school would love and envy. Not only that, had she not disappeared, she would have finished her school years with honors. How could she not? She had the undivided attention and care of two mothers. She pleased Soledad by wearing the costumes she made for her. She stood patiently through the fittings. She participated in every parade that Soledad asked her to. And she kissed and hugged Esperanza, always clinging to her like a barnacle to the stilts of a dock.

Every morning, Esperanza and Soledad took turns writing notes to put in Blanca's lunch bag. *When the juice of this mango drips down your arm, think of how much I love you.* Blanca collected every note in an envelope she kept in the diary she hid under her mattress. When Esperanza began sorting through her daughter's things after the funeral, she found the diary. She cried so much that the tears blurred her vision. She had to wait two weeks before she could read a word, but once she started, she read the entire thing in one sitting. Under other circumstances, she would not have violated Blanca's privacy. But now that she was gone, Esperanza went through the pages tracing the handwriting with her finger. She cherished the roundness of the o's, the firmness of the t's, and how the a's at the end of words curved the serif upward, almost touching the line above. Esperanza kissed nearly every word in the diary, even those that were misspelled, then put the diary back in its place.

On Tuesdays and Fridays, after school, Blanca had practiced guitar with her teacher, Don Remigio Montaño, a retired mariachi who helped her develop a passion for music. Before she was even seven years old she had already learned to play and sing a couple of boleros, without really understanding what the sad, heartbroken lyrics meant. Her little voice filled the house, floated out the window, and blended with the street noises, making the sound of a truck passing by not only bearable but harmonious.

But now she was gone. Now Soledad would have to

finish the dress for someone else, the sixteen-year-old daughter of one of Soledad's cousins, who would ruin the costume three summers later while being chased by her boyfriend in a sugarcane field, ultimately surrendering and making love with him in the mud.

While Soledad rocked mechanically on the chair in the portico, Esperanza sat inside, on Blanca's bed. She was angry at Soledad for not believing in San Judas Tadeo's apparition. And by not believing, Soledad's life after Blanca's disappearance had become one of grief, acceptance, and resignation, as if the girl were really dead.

With the palm of her hand, Esperanza ironed a crease on the bedspread and remembered how she had cleaned Blanca's room meticulously before she went to pick her up at the hospital. She had placed half a dozen white roses in a crystal vase and had set it on her night table, right next to a picture of Luis in a small silver frame. With respect, she had lit a brand-new candle, the kind that smelled like roses. She had pulled the sheets open, folding them out in a perfect triangle, and fluffed the pillow just the way Blanca liked. Soledad had come in the room, cooling off her sweaty face with a paper fan, minimizing the effects of the heatwave and an early menopause. She had hung the Jarocha costume from the rod by the window and fixed the flounces and frills. In four more months she would finish the embroidery along the sleeves and on the apron. But the rest of the dress was almost completed. She had planned it so that it could grow with Blanca, leaving enough fabric along the hem to let out as needed. This way, she could wear it to her Quince Años dance three years from now. Esperanza and Soledad had made sure every stitch was in the right place. They imagined the girl in it, dancing with the most handsome boy in town, waving the spacious white skirt like a storm at sea and making him dizzy from glimpses of her legs during the split seconds the skirt was up.

Blanca's clothes were still in the armoire. Her shoes were under her bed. Her dolls were on the pillow. The Jarocha dress still hung from the rod. She would not wear it. She would not make any boy dizzy from desire. She would not be kissed or adored. She would not marry or have children. Unless Esperanza found her.

August 4
Dear Diary,

I didn't want to get up today, but I did as soon as I remembered that I promised Ramona I would bring my mouse Pancho to school. I put him in the deep pocket my godmother had stitched under my uniform skirt so I can hide candy from Miss Norma in case I get hungry in class.

Pancho is so cute! Sometimes I'd like to set him free. I imagine him running around the sugarcane fields, nibbling on roots, moving his whiskers to com-

municate with fellow mice. I can't stand seeing him
locked up. Remember when I opened my godmother's
love birds' cage and they flew away? I almost got
spanked for that one. But it was worth it seeing them
perched up on the electrical wires across the street. My
guitar teacher gave those birds to her. He said,
"Soledad, I don't want to see you so lonely anymore."
I told her I think he likes her but she denies it.

  Pancho is mine and I can let him go if I wish.
Today he almost got away. I didn't feel it when he
crawled out of my pocket and went straight to sniff
Miss Norma's feet. I was so scared. I imagined her
jumping on the desk, screaming. But when she felt
Pancho's tiny pink paws on her ankle, she grabbed
him by the tail and asked, "Whose is it?" I got up,
waiting for my punishment. Pancho waited for his fate
as well, dangling in the air with his legs stiff and
spread out. She came really close to me and said, "I
had one just like him when I was little." Then she
kept him the rest of the day. Pancho crawled all over
her dress and she fed him crumbs from her cornbread.
When I told my mom this afternoon, she said she'd get
one to give to Miss Norma. Just because she's a grown-
up doesn't mean she can't have a white mouse for a
pet. Celestino, the boy I like, agrees with my mom. He
says Miss Norma should have a pet mouse of her own
and keep it in the classroom. I don't know about that.
The principal is not an animal lover. Good-bye. Talk
to you tomorrow.

                                                      Blanca

"I'm sorry I've come so late, Father Salvador, but I was in charge of closing the hardware store tonight. I'm Esperanza Díaz, the woman who's been talking to San Judas Tadeo. If I tell you that it happened again, you won't mention it to anyone? I know it's your job to keep secrets, but after what happened with Soledad, I have to make sure no one knows about the miracle. You knew very well what you were saying when you asked me to keep all this to myself, Father. She didn't believe me. I told her that so many years of praying must somehow pay off. It's like when you buy lottery tickets all your life. One day you get the grand prize. God squeezes, but He doesn't strangle. Still, she thinks I'm going crazy.

"This time I was making stuffed chicken breasts. I closed the oven door, and right away I checked the window. I moved my head this way and that to get a better look at the grease drippings, until, suddenly, there he was, talking to me, calling me by name. He said, 'Esperanza, you must find your daughter. Find her. No matter what you have to do. She is not dead, she is . . .' I tried touching the image and whispered, 'Where?' but he disappeared without giving me more specific instructions.

"I never told you about the last time I saw Blanca, did I? The day after her surgery, her girlfriend Ramona came by the hospital. She brought her school notebooks so

Blanca could catch up. They talked about their boy-friends. Now, Father, I'm sure they were imaginary, so don't worry. The girls exchanged some stickers with hearts and flowers. They were laughing so hard, the nurse came in to quiet them down. I knew Blanca was recovering fast. Her throat didn't hurt anymore.

"After Ramona left, I went home to prepare Blanca's bedroom and then downtown to get her a brooch I had been wanting to give her since she started seventh grade. A brooch a little too sophisticated for a twelve-year-old girl, but I knew she'd love it precisely because of that. It was made of silver filigree with turquoises and three pearls in the shape of tears hanging from a golden post. Around two o'clock, I returned to the hospital to pick her up.

"I have never been able to find my way around that hospital. Have you been to it, Father? You know, the General Hospital number 114, on the corner of Independencia and Revolución. That's where I saw my daughter last. It's big and crowded. I walked down a hallway, a bit disoriented, and for a moment I thought someone was following me. I was nervous. I hid in a closet. The footsteps went by. The light was dim. Among the brooms and cleaning rags, a fetus the size of my hand lay on a stainless steel tray. Just there, without a soul, not even missing the life it would not live. I didn't want to disturb it. I ran out into the hallway again. The patients walked slowly. Hurting. Recovering. Dying.

"I finally found a nurse's station and I asked a receptionist, 'Where can I pay? I'm here to pick up my daughter.' She was busy chewing on a pencil. She asked,

'What's the patient's name?' And I said, 'Blanca Díaz, I'm her mother.' She looked for Blanca's name on a pad. I said, 'She had her tonsils out.' She grabbed a clipboard hanging from a nail on the wall behind her and started flipping through the pages. Suddenly, the woman's skin seemed to lose its texture and color. Her face became transparent and wet, slippery and shiny. She stared at me fearfully, as one would look at someone about to be killed by a firing squad. She took the pencil out of her mouth. I tried to read the list, but the pad was upside down. She said, trembling, 'Ma'am, weren't you notified?'

"That's when I knew something was wrong. She sent me to the second floor to talk to Dr. Ortiz, but I went straight to where I had left Blanca instead. I ran so fast. I bumped into patients. I opened every possible door along the way, until finally, I found two nurses wearing surgical masks and latex gloves. They were spraying disinfectant on the bed where Blanca had been. Where was she?

"I searched the corridor until finally I heard Dr. Ortiz's voice coming from behind a door. I burst into the room. He was examining a patient with a skin problem. I asked the doctor, 'Where is my Blanca?' Oh, Father, you know what he said? He said, 'Mrs. Díaz, we don't know what happened, but your daughter passed away.' And that's all I remember. I collapsed in the patient's arms, and the next thing I knew, I was coming to in the emergency room.

"When I opened my eyes, Soledad's face was very close to mine and it looked blurry. From the look in her eyes, I knew she had found out about Blanca. She said,

'When I got here they told me. They have her at the morgue.' Her words sounded rehearsed, like an old movie soundtrack coming from a neighbor's TV set on one of those summer afternoons filled with clouds of mosquitoes spilling over Tlacotalpan. I had heard words like those many times at the theater, and now that they were referring to my own daughter, they didn't seem much different. I went numb. I felt I was living someone else's life, my brain telling me, 'Esperanza, you stay out of this.' Maybe San Judas Tadeo was taking care of things. Maybe he didn't want me to suffer because he already knew that Blanca wasn't dead. Then again, you may find this odd, Father, but when Luis was killed, my feelings became foreign, too, and the pain took its time sinking in.

"Nothing moved in the emergency room except my hand. I reached for a cotton ball soaked in alcohol and lightly touched my nose. An unexplained pressure on my chest didn't allow me to take deep breaths. A nurse gave me a shot. 'You'll feel better,' she said. The seconds grew into hours. It seemed as if I wasn't really there. I suffered from some kind of insomnia, the kind that fills the eyes with sand. I couldn't cry. My tear ducts must have been clogged. Soledad's hand crushed mine harder and harder until it hurt. That's when I finally got up and followed a nurse to the morgue, my mouth dry with the aftertaste of disbelief.

"The morgue was a windowless pale green room. I will never forget the smell. Formaldehyde, blood and sweat, together with the smell of tamale. Someone had been eating there just before we arrived.

"They gave us a sealed casket, Father. A coffin I would never have bought for my own daughter. It wasn't pink. It didn't have silk roses on the cover. No white taffeta padding around the edges. It wasn't adorned with laces and bows on the sides. It didn't even have a frame to put her picture in or a bone-carved crucifix. It was a simple pinewood box wrapped in clear sterile plastic. I rubbed the surface, tracing imaginary circles around the deep-driven nails, as if I could erase them.

"The nurse said we couldn't see Blanca. Even though I had been presented with this so-called coffin, I asked if she had been cremated. I know that the only mortuary in town does not have the equipment yet, but I couldn't think of another reason why I was not able to see her body. The nurse did not answer. She asked us to wait for the doctor and didn't even say please. If I hadn't been sedated by the shot I got at the emergency room, I would have hurt that woman, Father. I would have punched her right in the stomach. How could she be so rude?

"I borrowed Soledad's fan for a minute to cool off. Soledad dropped on the only chair, exhausted. I returned her fan and leaned over Blanca's coffin. The silence flew around us, flapping its noiseless wings like a hungry vulture.

"I needed more air. I wanted to be back in my mother's womb. I wished I could hold my husband's hand, may he rest in peace. I stared at an unimportant spot on the wall for I don't know how long. It seemed like hours until Dr. Ortiz walked in. I asked him to open the casket, but he said, 'I'm sorry to have to say no, Mrs. Díaz, but we don't know what she died from. It was so sudden, we believe it's a very contagious disease, some virus we still don't have a name for, and we can't risk starting an epidemic. The mortuary already has orders not to open the casket. She must be buried today.' I just blew my nose and tossed the tissue on the floor. Can you believe it, Father? How can a doctor give such a poor excuse?

"I pulled at the plastic and yanked on one of the thick nails in the coffin, but it was hammered tight. The words 'Do Not Open—Danger—Contagious' were scribbled with black marker across the top of the casket. The men from the mortuary finally came. They had me sign papers. I put my name next to the 'X' on more than a dozen documents. I always read what I sign. Every widow should. But this time I didn't. I just wanted to see Blanca, so I got really mad at the doctor. I'm sorry, Father. I know I shouldn't have done that. I said to him, 'Every time you doctors don't have an answer, you blame it on a virus. Murderer!' I grabbed his coat and pulled him. I hit him. He pushed me. Soledad ran around us screaming until she and the nurse were able to pull me away. Sweating, Dr. Ortiz left the room. I took the brooch out of my purse and gave it to Soledad. I said to her, 'Get rid of this, please. We don't need it anymore.'

"I have been trying to make sense of this second apparition. Afterward, as I was sitting on the kitchen floor by the oven and puzzling over San Judas Tadeo's instructions, Soledad came in from the market. I hadn't realized that the whole room was full of smoke, but she noticed it right away. She put the grocery bags on the counter and quickly took the charred stuffed chicken breasts out of the oven. Even though she's messy, she has always been efficient. I started crying, not so much for the burned food but for Blanca. How am I going to find her? Soledad opened the windows to let the smoke out and threw the food in the garbage. My cat Dominga looked in to see if there was anything worth rescuing, but there wasn't. That's when I told Soledad about San Judas Tadeo's second apparition. I told her about the oven and the grease drippings and the whole thing. And you know what she said? 'I understand we're very sad for what happened to Blanca, and sometimes we imagine things.' I'm sure she wanted to be delicate with my feelings. But then she went on, 'Don't you think our saint is too busy performing more important miracles than to appear before someone like you?'

"Well, that did it, Father. She's not in this with me. I gave her two chances. I realize now that I have to find Blanca by myself. And I feel bad that I've had to cause a little trouble along the way. I admit I made a pretty unpleasant scene at the Civil Registry office. But it wasn't on purpose. I was only following the orders of my saint. The Birth and Death Certificates official, a half-bald man with a belly hanging over his belt, was sitting at his metallic desk, which was old, filthy, and covered by a broken glass repaired with masking tape. I couldn't help noticing, under the glass, several magazine clippings of naked women. Excuse me, Father, I'm just telling you what I saw. When I asked him to issue an order to exhume Blanca's body on behalf of San Judas Tadeo, he said, 'I'm sorry, but I cannot authorize this.

Not even if the order came from God Almighty Himself. If the coroner's forensic service doesn't approve the exhumation, we can't dig up even the tiniest little bone.'

"Now, Father, don't get me wrong. It's not that I was questioning the words of San Judas Tadeo, but if Blanca is not in her grave, who did I bury? The casket was heavy, but it could have been full of rocks. So I insisted and the bureaucrat tried to walk me out the door. He said he had somebody waiting to meet with him, but I didn't see anyone. That's when I lost my patience. I yelled, 'If she were your daughter, you'd be digging with your fingernails!' and I pushed over a huge stack of documents piled up on his desk, spreading them all over the dusty floor. 'A year's worth of work!' he screamed. He tried to throw me out of his office, but I grabbed his arm and bit it until it bled. I'm sorry I did that, Father. You might want to treat it as a separate sin, I don't know; it's a suggestion. When I saw the little drops of blood on his shirtsleeve, I realized my reaction had been excessive, but it was too late. A reporter who was snooping around heard the screams and came running. He took my picture just when I was launching a big metal wastebasket full of paper onto the bureaucrat's desk, smashing the glass into pieces. No masking tape could do the job this time. I had to laugh, Father, looking at all those provocative women, oblivious to my pain, still trapped under the shards.

"Then a policeman came. He must have thought I was crazy. He grabbed me and pushed me out of the building, threatening to arrest me if he saw me again. I stumbled on the front steps, lost a shoe, and fell. While lying on the sidewalk, I figured, 'Why do I need permits if I have orders from higher up?' I got up in front of all the pedestrians, picked up my purse, put on my shoe, and limped home. My pride is all right, but my ankle still hurts.

"I'll let you go now, Father. You must have things to do tonight. I just want you to keep in mind, when you give me my penance, that I'm very sorry I'm causing trouble. I will let you know if San Judas Tadeo appears before me again. In the name of the Father and of the Son and of the Holy Ghost. Amen."

Oh God, dear God. How am I supposed to guide this woman from a confessional box? You heard her. She comes to me and tells me what she's done, not what she will do. I understand that's what confessions are all about, but then I have no way of stopping her. Maybe I shouldn't. I've been waiting for her to return since her last confession. I look for her in church. I can't sleep thinking what she might be doing. Is she speaking to San Judas Tadeo again? Is she ironing a pile of clothes? Is she punching a government employee in the nose? I anticipate her next confession. I need to hear her voice through the cloth on my confessional box window. The way she whispers into my ears her story of anguish and

horror and determination, my forehead gets all sweaty. I
have to set my little electric fan on high, the one I have
installed right on the ceiling next to the lightbulb. I even
forget to cough. Her presence is an invitation to think
about Consuelo.

I know. I promised You thirty-six years ago, or is it
thirty-seven? I can't remember. But I haven't forgotten
that I vowed to You I would not mention her name
again. I thought that You might be tired of hearing me
tell You I loved her since I was a boy. My mother never
knew that my nana Consuelo came to my room every
night to tuck me in and caress my body until I was as
hard as a corn cob. She'd kiss me, tell me stories and sing
me songs, my head resting on her breast, until I pretended to fall asleep. Then she'd go to the maid's quarters in the small house by the orchard, at the edge of the
property, and make love with her husband, the gardener.
I'd follow her quietly and wait outside the window until
I heard the bed squeaking and her moaning. Then I'd
return home and try to sleep. One summer night, when
I had just finished sixth grade, right after we said our
nightly prayers and made the sign of the cross, I slid my
hand under her skirt. I don't know if You were there
watching us or not. She was twenty-four. I unbuttoned
her blouse. Her womb had never carried a child. I took
off my shirt. Aside from moments in my dreams, this
was the first time I touched her nipple with the tip of my
tongue. She spread her body over me, naked and warm.
A crib blanket, tucking her arms under my shoulders.
For hours we appeared and disappeared in the shadows
of my room. We were a yes-and-no contradiction, a sin

without contrition. Before dawn, she said, "You will dream about little angels fluttering around you," and went back to her quarters.

The next morning, my father discovered that she and her husband had left without giving notice. He thought that they might have stolen something from him. We searched for clues among the few belongings they had left behind. A shirt. A tote bag. A right shoe. Secretly, I hoped to find a forwarding address, but all that was left of value were her scents. The bedspread, the pillow, the curtains, the doorknob. They all had been impregnated with the smell of warm tortillas, of fresh-cut tomatillos, of cilantro. Since then, I've made love with no one else and You know that. When I told my father, a few years later, that I wished to join the seminary, he stopped speaking to me. My seven sisters agreed that my father's punishment, in return, was that my vow of celibacy ensured that his name would die out. Now he is up there with You in Heaven, and I am sure he is aware of everything that went on. I hope You have forgiven him for punishing me with his silence. Sometimes I still have dreams that there's a child of mine somewhere being brought up by Consuelo, a child who bears my name. That would probably help my father rest in peace: At least he'd know what Consuelo had stolen from him.

I thought I had forgotten about her. But the desire, the desperate need to hold Esperanza against my body and feel her warmth, has brought her back. I'm sorry I'm telling You this, but who else can I talk to? If my love for a woman directed me to the priesthood, my love for another woman could guide me out. I'm scared. What can a confused, fifty-six-year-old priest do? Esperanza is unstoppable. She's on a mission. It's Your will. All I can do is pray for her. Am I wrong to believe her?

Esperanza wrapped a bandage tight around her ankle, thinking how easily physical pain diminished. She'd have to put away her high-heeled shoes for a few days and borrow Blanca's sandals. She used to like wearing them on Sundays when they went to the river to fish for fresh-water prawns. Just a couple of months before, they had all spent the day by the shore. Soledad didn't swim, but she liked to take pictures. From the water, she seemed like a big tent about to be blown away by the wind. Her wide hips filled her ample orange skirt. She couldn't hold her umbrella and take a picture at the same time, but at least one good snapshot of Blanca always came out of every roll of film.

Blanca was Soledad's main subject. She had over twenty photo albums filled with pictures of the girl since she was a baby. Learning to dance the jarana for the Independence Day parade, walking up to her knees in water when the river flooded the streets, getting her guitar for Christmas when she was barely three, fixing the rocking chair armrest on the portico, kissing Esperanza on her birthday. Almost as if Soledad knew that someday soon those photos would be all she had left of her goddaughter.

The three of them could have stayed all day at the river, but if they didn't go to Mass before four, they'd be eaten by the mosquitoes that loved the cool air circulating under the white pews of the church. So they rode their bikes home, carrying a basketful of prawns for dinner. On the way, Esperanza noticed two teenage boys following them and giggling and pushing each other. Blanca slowed her bike down slightly. The boys hid behind a parked car. She turned her head to see if they were still there and smiled at them. The boys ran inside a magenta house with green doors and windows. She knew who they were.

"The one in the yellow shirt goes to my school. His name is Celestino. He wants to marry me when I'm eighteen," Blanca said to her mother.

Esperanza had stopped her bike and pretended to rearrange the squirming prawns in the basket. She didn't want to discover in her daughter's eyes even the slightest look of love. I got married at that age, she had thought, terrified. But then again, Blanca was still a little girl. There was no way she could be thinking about boys just yet.

Esperanza limped to their room and looked for the sandals under Blanca's bed. A Jarocha doll leaned on the pillow, its beautiful little costume made to size by Soledad herself, with a circular white skirt, an embroidered black apron, and a spectacular headpiece, made stiff by starch. The two beds were so close to each other that mother and daughter could hold hands at night whenever a thunderstorm hit Tlacotalpan. They slept separated only by a night table with a lamp, Luis' picture, and a permanently lit candle.

Blanca's sandals were still there, along with a few other pairs of shoes. Esperanza tried the sandals on. They fit snugly, more so on her left foot, around the bandage. Just then she remembered seeing Celestino, the boy in the yellow shirt, sitting on a grave at Blanca's funeral, away from the crowd, staring at the priest and rocking his body slowly to the rhythm of the windless day. She hadn't paid much attention to him. Too many people had gone to the service.

Esperanza remembered where the boy lived and suddenly wanted to visit him and tell him that Blanca was alive. That she would find her. That he could marry her in six more years. She walked slowly out of her house, careful not to hurt her ankle, and headed to the magenta house with the green doors and windows. But she stopped when she reached the Callejón de los Delfines. She could see Celestino's house from that narrow alley but turned back before walking up to the portico. She could not talk to him. She had no idea how she would find Blanca. Not yet. So she went home again, using a back street to avoid limping in front of the Civil Registry office.

Blanca's diary was in the same place Esperanza had left it the day she read it from cover to cover. She lifted the mattress and pulled it out, careful not to damage it. Perhaps if she read it again she would find more meanings to her daughter's words, secret symbols she'd have to decode using the power of her motherly nature. She wanted to read again and look for answers, clues. Maybe she had missed an important detail, from reading too fast. There had to be more than words in those pages.

August 28
Dear Diary,

   It's been a week since I wrote anything. I have been very busy practicing for my guitar recital next month, but I just had to make some time to write this. I'm confused. A couple of days ago, Celestino walks me home from school and we stop by the dock to get ice cream. Avocado for him. Pistachio for me. We sit on the loading platform's steps for a while. As we talk, he gets closer and closer and finally he puts his arm around me. He asks me if I want to taste his ice cream and then touches my lips with his tongue. I like it so much (his tongue, not the ice cream) that I let him lick my lips. Then he tells me again that he wants to marry me in a few years. Now what am I going to say to him? I can't allow this to happen again. Ramona says I could get pregnant from a kiss. Even if I haven't

gotten my first period yet. But I really liked it. One
thing is for sure: I can't tell my mom.

> *I wish you could talk.*
> *Blanca*

"Father Salvador, I want to thank you right here in front of God for agreeing to listen to my confession at this early hour. Good thing you were already up. I couldn't sleep, and if I didn't talk to you before six o'clock Mass, I wouldn't have been able to come until tonight after work, and I don't know if I could have waited that long.

"You probably wonder where I've been these days. Well, I have been thinking how am I going to find Blanca. After I read her diary—I'm her mother and it's for her own safety that I did it—it occurred to me she might have eloped with Celestino, a boy from her school, but I went to his house and there he was. He wept when he saw me at the door. I didn't tell him that Blanca is not dead. Not until I find her. I just asked him how he was doing. He went inside and came back with a little medal of the Virgen de Guadalupe that belonged to Blanca. I told him he could keep it. Then I went back to the hospital to look for Dr. Ortiz and see if he could help me get permission from the forensic service to dig up Blanca's coffin. I hoped that by now he would forgive me for being so impolite at the morgue.

"The glass door, all marked with greasy fingerprints, refused to open. Or maybe I was reluctant to go in. I had to wait for two nurses to open it. They must have sensed something, because one of them asked if I was all right. I said, 'It's just my ankle that hurts.' They looked at the bandage, realized my case was no emergency, and walked away. My ankle wasn't what hurt the most, but why should they know about my pain?

"I walked to the reception desk and asked a nurse sitting there about Dr. Ortiz. She said he didn't work there anymore. She believed he had gotten sick and his family had taken him to Mexico City. She started cleaning her bifocals. I asked her if she knew his relatives' address. She didn't. I had heard that he wasn't from our town. He comes from Sonora or some state up north. I have to speak with him, Father. He's the only person who can get me the permit. Then she said, 'Well, they say he passed away, but I'm not sure. Can some other doctor help you?' I didn't know what to say. She looked concerned. So I asked her when he resigned and she looked at a calendar. Can you believe it, Father? He disappeared the same day Blanca died. How do you explain that? I stayed up all night thinking, making connections between events. Oh, Father, I even find it hard to say it, but I'm sure this is what happened: He took her. There's no other explanation. He must have abducted her for child prostitution. It's easy for a doctor to stage a girl's death in a hospital and then sell her to a brothel in another town. I've read articles about this in the paper before. There is a whole underground industry. They say thirty thousand people disappear each year! That's the entire population of Tlacotalpan. Imagine that. Everything makes sense now. That's why San Judas Tadeo has sent me to look for her. He knows she is in danger.

"I've been praying to San Pafnucio, patron of lost things and people. I put his statuette on top of a magnifying glass by the window facing north. I have invoked Santa Úrsula, patron of girls, and Santa Alodia, patron of child abuse victims, to look after Blanca, wherever she might be. I need all their help, and I ask you to pray as well, if you please. Your voice must stand out among the millions of prayers shooting up to the sky every day. And I also want to offer a Mass for Blanca. You'll say to the congregation it's for her soul, but only you and I will know it's for her safe return. Will you do it? I will be grateful to you forever. In the name of the Father and of the Son and of the Holy Ghost. Amen."

Oh, my God, my dear God. What am I going to do with Esperanza? Child prostitution, of all things. The doctor could have gotten sick from the same virus. I offered to find out the truth at the hospital, but she was certain he had kidnapped the girl. How is she going to find her? She can't go to the authorities. They won't believe her story. All I said was, "Be careful." It's my duty as a priest. I can only plead with her not to get in trouble. She must learn to interpret San Judas Tadeo's messages. The problem is that I can't teach her. I have never seen an apparition. You must have a reason for depriving me of that privilege. As much as I've wished for it to happen in all my years of service to You, I still haven't experienced the slightest sign from Heaven.

When I was five years old I thought You had sent me one. The illusion happened on a cold Sunday. I think I've told You this before. See how I'm starting to forget things? I had a fever but I went to church with my mother anyway. I sat by her quietly. The priest's steady murmur almost lulled me to sleep, and I suddenly saw a winged man of many colors materializing on the marble floor in front of me. He was so beautiful I thought I had died and was being welcomed into Your house. But the following week I realized that the angel was only the reflection of the stained-glass window on the floor as the sunlight came through. I'm still waiting. I've come to believe it is a test of faith. You said it, "Those who believe without seeing will live forever in My Kingdom." Well, that's me. Perhaps I should be grateful for Your silence.

Now I have to give advice to a woman on how to interpret her saint's words, and I have as little experience with that as I do with lovemaking, but still I teach couples how to love each other. Don't You realize that in this confessional box I am the one who learns? And I don't get to practice. Wish me luck, dear God. Amen.

Esperanza wouldn't normally have gone out of her house alone so late at night. The street looked different, wider and lacking color. She had a brand-new shovel in her hand, the price tag from Los Valerosos hardware store still taped to the handle. Barely any noises surrounded her. Even the crickets knew they should be respectful that particular evening and kept from their usual chatter.

At the cemetery, Esperanza pushed the heavy iron gate until she was finally able to sneak in through a narrow opening. She was careful not to make any movements that might draw attention, but two hungry stray dogs heard her and came running. One was brown and had a few white spots. His yellow eyes seemed to beg for food. The other was long, but his legs were short. He reminded Esperanza of a dinner table she had once had. She had its legs cut in half to make a coffee table, but it never looked quite right.

"Get out of here!" she whispered.

The dogs began sniffing her skirt. She paid no attention and headed straight to Blanca's grave. They followed her.

The cemetery was crowded with family members who had gone to a better life. Hardly any space was left, but people did not like to bury their dead relatives in the new cemetery outside of town, though it had been well planned and had a beautiful view of the river. The new place was filled with loneliness and the deceased hated that feeling. If they were buried there, they would not be close to their ancestors. An unforgiving act. Everyone knew that families must stay together even after death. In the old graveyard, mausoleums were so close to one another that people could come and visit every dead family member at the same time. That's what Esperanza did Sunday after Sunday. Her parents' tombs were only a few steps away from her husband's, and now, Blanca's grave. She and Soledad would take their lunch in a basket and sit on the tombstones to chat and bring their loved ones up to date on who was marrying whom, who had a baby, who was not speaking to whom, and, of course, as if the dead didn't already know, who had passed away.

It was difficult for Esperanza to find her way at night. During the day, she knew that to get to Blanca's grave she had to make a left past the Garcías' mausoleum, painted in California poppy orange. Then a right at the Salazars', in a Jell-O lime green. And just before reaching the back wall, she had to make another right at the Mendozas', that one a bathroom-tile blue. But the moon was covered by dark clouds and did not bring out the colors, so Esperanza took a few wrong turns before she got to where, supposedly, her daughter's remains were not resting in peace.

Blanca's grave was plain, with a temporary wooden cross as a marker. Written on the cross, in Esperanza's hand, were the words "In memory of Blanca Díaz. In case she is here." Esperanza had been putting off building a big cement mausoleum, painted bright pink and with a glass window in which to place Blanquita's picture and a candle.

Esperanza began digging. The dogs sat by her to watch. Fortunately, the soil was still loose. Unfortunately, it started to rain.

"You're getting wet for no reason!" she told the dogs, keeping her voice down and systematically shoveling mud out of the grave, but really she was talking to herself. She was scared of finding Blanca there. She was also scared of not finding her.

The rains came to Tlacotalpan every summer, making the river swell and flooding the streets up to people's knees. For two weeks, everyone raised their furniture on upside-down tin buckets, tied their drapes up in knots, rolled up their rugs, sloshed through water, and waited for the river to shrink back to its normal size before they started to clean up. Esperanza herself had become an experienced flood survivor. At age six, the river had taken her father, but she and her mother, who were in church at the time, made it safely to the bell tower. And because they prayed to San Adjutor, patron saint invoked against drowning, her father's body was one of the few that were found, right next to the bloated corpse of a bull. Now Esperanza's whole house was prepared to receive half a meter of water, year after year, without harming the sofas, tables, chairs, and beds. In a matter of forty-five minutes, every single thing she possessed could be safe, up high. She didn't even need to conduct drills anymore. But that night she was not in her house and the rain began to pour, turning the cemetery soil into a viscous, sticky, drippy mud.

"San Isidro, please, don't make it harder on me, for God's sake!" she pleaded, her face soaking wet.

But her saint, patron of rain and weather, did not listen. Perhaps he couldn't hear because of the loud noise the downpour made. The hole was getting deeper. She began digging faster. The dogs sat at the edge of the grave.

"Don't even think we're going to find bones here, if that's what you're waiting for. Go on! Get out!" She scared them off with stones but they kept coming back.

Sinking deeper and deeper into the grave, she dug all night. Her arms went numb. She couldn't tell which drops were rain and which were sweat. No matter how fast she shoveled mud out, creeks of turbid water poured back into the hole, until she hit something hard. The casket. She dug with her hands. She wanted them to be the first thing to touch her daughter, if she was in there. She reached for the lid of the casket, the plastic seal now broken, but the nails still held it shut. Her hands were boiling with blisters. The rain became a timid drizzle. She thanked San Isidro for the favor. He had proved himself again as the ultimate patron saint of the rain and poor weather conditions. She made the sign of the cross. She knocked on the wood and stood still, as if waiting for an answer. She knocked again. The coffin sounded as hollow as a drum.

San Judas Tadeo is right, Blanca is not buried here, she is somewhere else. The coffin is empty, she thought. She kneeled on top of the casket and prayed, "Please, San Judas Tadeo, give me the strength to look for

Blanca, wherever she might be. You've given me enough evidence to know she is not buried here. I entrust you with my life, my spirit, my will. I'll find her, no matter what. I'll do what I have to do. Your orders are clear. And please forgive me for second-guessing you. But I just had to make sure."

As she began climbing out of the hole, Esperanza noticed in the distance two straight lines of light slashing the night. The dogs began to bark at the darkness.

"Didn't I tell you? They're over here!" said someone.

Esperanza was still inside the hole when the light of a flashlight hit her face. Two men slipping in the mud, one young, the other old, appeared above her and knelt to pull her out of the grave.

"You're going straight to jail, lady," said the old man.

The short-legged dog barked, threatening to bite the young man, but received a kick in the snout that sent him down with Esperanza.

"Go rob stuff from the living. At least they can defend themselves," said the young man.

"This piece of land is my property!" she cried. "I paid for it in perpetuity!"

But the guards didn't listen. They clasped her arms. She refused to move. They were strong and finally pulled her out onto the muddy grass. She wasn't going to let them stop her. She couldn't look for Blanca locked up in jail. She yanked herself away, but they trapped her again, talking over her incoherent screams and dragging her across the cemetery toward the gate.

"If I were you," said the older man to the young man in a calm voice, "I'd go see Don Chon before going to the doctor. When I had this fart problem, he operated on me by just putting a cotton ball with some alcohol right on my belly. No scalpel. No surgery at all."

Esperanza screamed, kicked, bit. No use. The older man gagged her with a handkerchief.

"And what was it? What did you have?" said the young man.

"Gas. Just pure fucking gas for telling so many lies to my old lady," answered the older man. "My whole intestine was bloated." He clutched Esperanza's wrists with all his strength.

"And he didn't prescribe anything?"

"Just suck on a sugarcane after every lie I tell my old lady. I swear to God, there's a remedy for everything, you just have to go to the right person."

Esperanza's screams were muffled by the man's handkerchief. She noticed the dogs following her, and wondered how the short-legged one had managed to climb out of the hole.

"Do I need an appointment?" The young man showed a great deal of interest in the old man's advice.

"No. You just show up. You'll see, Don Chon will get rid of those warts on your tongue."

"You really think so?"

As the men continued to drag Esperanza through the cemetery, branches along the way scratched her legs. Bruises bloomed on her wrists. Her foot became stuck between two tombstones. The men pulled her until it finally came free, but she lost her shoe.

They hauled her all the way to the gate, but just when they were about to cross it, Esperanza freed herself and ran outside, closing a huge padlock around the iron bars and leaving the men inside to look for the key in their pockets.

She ran in the deepest darkness, the kind that announces daybreak is imminent, until suddenly she realized she had left the shovel behind. They could track her down with that kind of evidence. To retrieve it, she'd have to wait for the guards to leave. She hid under a parked truck outside the gate and listened to their conversation behind the cemetery wall. The dogs had followed her out of the graveyard and were now settling into her hiding place.

"Grave robbers. A fucking pain, I'm telling you," Esperanza heard the young man say behind the wrought-iron gate, as she counted her injuries.

"Just leave her alone. She didn't take anything."

"You think we scared her?"

"Of course. Didn't you see her run? Only dead is she coming back."

The dogs licked Esperanza's face. She'd have to climb right back over the gate to get the shovel as soon as the men left. Six o'clock Mass was starting soon. Blanca's Mass. The Mass she'd requested Father Salvador to offer for her soul.

"He got rid of Don Enrique's warts. He got them for wanting to fuck Fermín González's wife," said the old man, his words fading in the distance.

"Oh, really?" asked the young man. "Did he end up fucking her?"

"Sure did. That was the prescription Don Chon gave him."

*   *   *

Esperanza's legs did not walk fast enough for her. The heel of her remaining shoe became stuck between the cobblestones of the narrow sidewalk and came off. She didn't stop to pick it up. But she did think Blanca's flat-heeled sandals would have been a better choice to wear at the cemetery. The dogs trotted with her all the way to the Candelaria Church, their fur drying off with the first rays of sun sneaking up behind the bell tower. She could hear a nasal song coming from inside the church: "Oh, Lord, You've seen my eyes and smiling You've said my name. On the sand, I've left my boat and by Your side, I'll find another ocean."

She had known the lyrics since she was a little girl, but for some reason she could not sing through her nose like the old ladies, as much as she tried. Six o'clock Mass was well under way. She hid the shovel behind a nearby hibiscus bush and warned the dogs to stay outside.

"Don't go anywhere. I may need you as witnesses."

The dogs sat obediently at the front steps as if they knew their place in the world.

Esperanza rubbed at the mud on her face, but she smeared it even more. She hoped God could see through the dirt. Limping, she walked into the ancient church. From the ceiling, images of cherubs, clinging to the last vestiges of peeled paint, followed Esperanza with their eyes.

She knelt at the end of the aisle and made the sign of the cross before taking a seat at the edge of the last pew. A lady, perhaps the oldest in Tlacotalpan, sat in front of her. She wore a Kleenex on her head in lieu of a veil and listened to the voice of Father Salvador as if carrying out the most painful sacrifice of her life. The saints trapped inside smudged glass cases, pinned to walls, dangerously keeping their balance on pillars all stared at Esperanza. She thought that if they talked like San Judas Tadeo had, they would probably reprimand her for showing up in church covered in dirt. But she couldn't miss her daughter's Mass.

"This Mass is dedicated to the soul of our sister Blanca Díaz, may she be sitting in Heaven by the side of our Lord." Father Salvador scanned the sparse congregation, furtively looking for Esperanza.

"This Mass is dedicated to the safe return of our sister Blanca Díaz, may she be sitting on a bus on her way home to her dear mother," whispered Esperanza.

The old lady overheard the supplication and turned around to see who had spoken, definitely not ready for the shock. Esperanza gave the woman her whitest smile and the woman, in turn, learned that even at her old age she could still be astonished by some people's shamelessness. She swallowed a cry of disgust and moved to another pew. Although Esperanza was already getting used to being seen with eyes of indignation, it wasn't in her plans to scare the elderly, so she got up quickly and took a seat in the shadows, behind a column.

Esperanza looked up at San Martín de Porres. He was small and dusty. The glass dome that had once protected him had smashed against the floor during the Córdoba earthquake and had never been replaced, leaving him at the mercy of the tropical breezes and moths that insisted on attacking his robe. Esperanza always thought that perhaps the reason San Martín de Porres was in such a sorry-looking state was because his broom attracted filth, just like the lightbulb in a taco stand attracted flies. She moved from her seat once more and knelt on a prie-dieu right under her saint and stared at him, trying to put together a few words that made sense. He stood there, on his little pedestal, patiently waiting for her to talk. San Martín de Porres. The only black saint Esperanza knew. In fact, the only black she knew. Period.

From the pulpit, Father Salvador warned the male parishioners again, "I know who is coveting his neighbor's wife. You know perfectly well who I'm talking about, and I want you all lined up here for confession next Sunday. I don't need to say it again."

He then coughed so much that Fidencio, the mute sacristan, got worried and ran up to help him. He couldn't say, "Raise your arms, Father, take a deep breath!" He could only pat him on the back until the priest could return to his speech.

Esperanza remembered the time she overheard a woman at a restaurant say that, thanks to a grammatical issue, only nine of the Commandments applied to women. Nowhere did it say, "Thou shall not covet thy neighbor's husband." Not that it mattered to her. After Luis passed away, she had never desired any man.

"You see?" Esperanza whispered to her saint. "Now I'm just as dark as you."

She smiled and the drying mud on her cheeks crackled.

"Look, San Martín, you're so good, so miraculous, you understand every language, please give this message to San Judas Tadeo: Tell him he was right. Tell him that

Blanca, my daughter, is not in her grave. Ask him what I should do next. I would ask him myself, but I don't want to go all the way to the front of the church like this. Everyone would see me and some people might get distracted from the Mass."

San Martín de Porres stood still, but Esperanza saw how his eyes turned in the direction of the statue of San Antonio de Padua, across the pews. She thanked San Martín de Porres for his guidance and tiptoed to the back of the church and around to the other side of the pews. Quietly, she knelt in front of San Antonio de Padua, patron of lost people and invoked by women who wished to get husbands.

San Antonio de Padua wore a blue velvet robe, faded and torn. Dozens of wedding photos and pictures of girls ready for marriage were pinned to his clothes. A wedding cake decoration of a bride and groom made out of sugar had a line of ants crawling all over it. On the wall behind the statue, some retablos, ex-votos, and votives showed illustrations of missing loved ones, others of old maids getting married. San Antonio de Padua held the child Jesus in his right arm, and a worn-out wax lilac flower in his left hand. Esperanza looked in her wallet, wet and muddy, and found a passport-size photo of Blanca. She fastened it to the saint's robe with a safety pin she picked up from the floor.

"San Antonio, you're so miraculous, you can find a grain of salt in a desert, so please help me find Blanca."

Esperanza lit a candle and dropped a coin into the offerings box slot. At that moment, as if activated by the coin like a kiddie ride, San Antonio de Padua turned his eyes to look at Esperanza. His face glowed. The lilac flower shrugged off its wax until the whole plant became natural, giving off a scent she could not identify, perhaps because there were no lilacs in Tlacotalpan. The old ladies singing and all other noises in the church faded away, leaving Esperanza alone with her saint until the Mass ended.

"In the name of the Father and of the Son and of the Holy Ghost. Amen. This Mass has ended, you may go in peace and love one another."

Father Salvador made the sign of the cross in the air and disappeared behind a side door. Esperanza hid from the congregation, kneeling on the prie-dieu and covering her face with her hands as if in intense prayer so she wouldn't alarm anyone else. When she heard no more footsteps, she looked around. She was alone, surrounded by statues of saints in pain.

"Thanks for giving me all this strength, San Antonio. I can feel it already. You are right. Blanca is a little grain of salt in the desert, but I have your help. I have the help of all my dear saints."

The saint's eyes had become marbles again. His lilac flower returned to wax. She kissed the saint's toe and hurried toward the side door.

The square open-air cloister, like many other areas of the church, had forgotten the meaning of the word maintenance. Its columns, nearly choked by a wild and unrestrained ivy that climbed around them, were slowly crumbling like two-day-old churros. The white paint on the walls was peeling, perhaps on purpose, to reveal faded colors underneath where there had been frescoes before. Cracked terra-cotta pots, their pieces held together with wire around their bases and at the tops, were placed symmetrically along the sides of the hallway, some of them too small for the overgrown geraniums they contained.

But not everything was dying. A constant murmur seemed to give life to the place. From the ceiling came the cooing of pigeons, unnoticed tenants who didn't care who walked along the cloister's corridors. Their droppings had always been democratic, sometimes hitting the worn-out limestone floor, sometimes hitting Fidencio, the mute sacristan, and, most frequently, Father Salvador. Occasionally, they peered down from their nests, built in the holes between the termite-infested beams, to see who was passing by. Most often, it was Father Salvador, who, from the pigeons' perspective, was a tall, robust aging man with a round and shiny almost-bald head painstakingly wrapped in long, grayish strands of hair. A perfect target.

This time, the human being running down the hallway was Esperanza, trying to catch up with the priest on his way to the kitchen.

"Father!" A cat leaped out of her path.

Father Salvador turned and saw her. He knew right then she had been to the cemetery.

"Father, please forgive me for coming to the house of God like this, but I must ask you if it's a sin to dig up a grave."

Esperanza embraced Father Salvador. She didn't

want to cry, but sometimes, very seldom, her feelings didn't obey her orders. He tried to say something, but his tongue felt stuck to the roof of his mouth.

"It's empty, Father. Such a big funeral, so much crying, so much pain, and I buried nothing."

Father Salvador stroked Esperanza's hair. He trembled, like an adolescent boy who tries to kiss a girl for the first time. He noticed his hand shaking and tried to control it by squeezing a length of her thick, dark hair.

To Esperanza, his caress reminded her of her own father and how he used to embrace her on the rocking chair when she was a girl. A feeling of comfort that she had learned to forget since the flood.

Both of them hugged so intensely, each in his own way, that neither of them heard the pigeons above. Their droppings kept missing them, except for one that dripped down Esperanza's shoulder. Even if she had noticed, she wouldn't have cared.

A timid morning breeze brought the humid smell of the river and pushed it through the cracks in the walls into the sacristy. The cloister filled with incomprehensible whispers rolling in tiny whirlwinds and repeating themselves in the most remote corners, but what Esperanza really needed were words. With substance. Finally Father Salvador said, "You believe. You will find her."

"Fidencio, yesterday morning, before breakfast, you saw me embracing Mrs. Díaz in the cloister. I noticed you hiding behind a column. Is that right? You don't have to answer me, even if you could, that is. Regardless of what you saw, it's not what you might be thinking. She is a parishioner in pain and my job as a priest is to help souls find peace. She needed to be held. She has lost her parents, her husband, and now her daughter. Some believers of the Catholic faith need words. Others need to be consoled with some kind of physical gesture, like a handshake, a hug, even a kiss. She needed both. Words and an embrace. The embrace of a brother. This is a difficult case for reasons I am not going to explain to you, but I ask you not to judge me by what you saw. And please, Fidencio, not a word of this to anyone. You know what I mean."

The hard-working Spanish immigrant known in town as Chilepanzón was Esperanza's boss at the hardware store, but his real name was Don Arlindo and that's what she called him. She learned that a way to keep a safe distance between herself and men was to treat them with absolute respect. By just saying "Don" before "Arlindo," she had put a thick wall between them that stopped him from kissing her as he threatened he would her first day on the job.

The morning of Blanca's Mass, two early-bird customers at the store were the first to notice Esperanza when she walked in, still covered with mud, shovel in hand. One of them pointed out to the other that she was wearing only one shoe and it had no heel. It had certainly paid for them to get up early. Now they'd have something new to talk about at coffee time. Esperanza limped in front of them and found Don Arlindo behind the counter. The dogs from the cemetery had followed her. They must have figured she'd be there a while because both of them lay down on the sidewalk and got to work swatting off flies with their tails.

"I'm sorry I took the shovel, Don Arlindo. You can take it off my paycheck. I just had to use one last night and I didn't have a shovel at home." Esperanza handed him the filthy tool.

"Look at you! Is this how you're supposed to show up to your job? Go home and change. We've got work to do."

"I can't work for you any longer. I have another commitment." She gave him a big, honest smile to diminish the impact of the news.

Don Arlindo hyperventilated every time he saw

Esperanza's smile, white from eating so many tortillas. This time, her teeth seemed even whiter in contrast to the mud on her face. From behind the counter, he pulled out the newspaper folded open to the page where Esperanza's photo appeared and waved it in her face. As much as he desired her, his anger made him forget that he had yellowish teeth from smoking so many cigars, and he showed them to her like a vicious baboon. If he couldn't love her, at least he'd hate her. Esperanza noticed a piece of cilantro stuck on Don Arlindo's front tooth.

"Is this your other commitment?"

Don Arlindo pointed to the photo showing Esperanza shattering the glass on the officer's desk at the Civil Registry office. She was surprised to see her face printed on the front page of *El Dictamen*. Everyone read that paper in town. In fact, it was the only one in the area. She imagined her neighbors talking about her, roaming outside her house, snooping through the windows.

"Or is it your family tragedy that has made you lose your mind?" he insisted.

Esperanza didn't answer. She left without saying good-bye. She didn't even thank him for the job he gave her for nine whole years. She did have work to do. Plenty of it. But not at the hardware store.

When she turned the corner, she bumped into Soledad, who had been looking for her since early morning. She had the newspaper clipping with Esperanza's photo inside a clear plastic sleeve. The word was definitely out.

"Thank God! Where were you?"

For some reason, since her husband's death, Soledad's voice never sounded normal. She always seemed apprehensive, even when she wasn't. But this time she was.

"This is getting out of hand, Esperanza," Soledad continued, using the newspaper clipping as a fan to cool off. "You spent the night out of the house." She was offended. "You've never done this before. You're even in the paper. What's the matter with you?"

"I went to help Father Salvador with the herb garden."

"I'd rather you not say anything. I hate lies."

Soledad looked around, making sure nobody watched them. She took off her shawl and wrapped Esperanza with it.

"For the sake of your dignity, Esperanza, you can't keep on doing this to yourself."

From her purse, Soledad took a tiny jar of Vicks VapoRub and dabbed some ointment around her nostrils, breathing deeply. She did that when she was tense and worried, although she attributed the habit to her allergies.

Esperanza didn't tell Soledad that she had been to the cemetery, that she had been chased by the guards, or that she'd quit her job, either. For the first time, a deep silence, the kind that hurts, settled between the two women.

"Father Salvador, I want to apologize for not coming to church last week. I'm really sorry. I've been thinking about you, though. I have prayed the twenty-five rosaries you gave me as a penance for digging up my daughter's grave. I even prayed a few more just in case you were more merciful with me than God would have liked. And I've thought of stopping by many times, but a lot of things have happened. This time I've brought you some pretty big sins. So huge, in fact, that I can't even fit them through my mouth. I had to quit my job. Well, that was really more of a blessing. Not that I don't like to work, but I need the time to look for Blanca. San Judas Tadeo has appeared before me two more times. The first time I was making baked potatoes with cream and ham. I won't go into details because I imagine you haven't had breakfast at this early hour and I don't want to make you hungry. Anyway, his image appeared in the stains on the oven window again and he said, 'Find her!' Where to start looking, Father? It's like looking for a cat's hair in a shag carpet. Dr. Ortiz must have her in one of those hotels that smell of sin where truck drivers stop for a beer and a . . . well, Father, I don't dare to say the other word to you, but that's what they're making Blanca do.

"You know what I mean, don't you? Many men have come to confess those sins, right? Not that you have to mention their names. Everybody ends up finding out anyway. I've heard there are people who kidnap girls and sell them to houses of sin, but I doubt you could tell me about it. I guess these people never make it to your confessional box. But they do exist. I read many cases in the newspaper. They must have her going through hell. And all I have are San Judas Tadeo's instructions. The last time he appeared before me, I could see his face clearly forming in the charred fat stuck to the oven window. The whole stove was shining as if the sun itself had traveled millions of miles to hide inside the little space where I bake my food. I thought of borrowing Soledad's camera and taking a picture. But I would have missed San Judas Tadeo if I'd gone to get it from her armoire. He's always in a rush. He said, 'You must get to her, no matter what! She is not dead . . .' I said, 'So, where is she? Tell me!' But instead of answering, he disappeared in his usual way, taking another little bit of brightness from my kitchen.

"He's not very communicative. I wish he'd give me more clues. I sat by the stove thinking how I could go about it, until it occurred to me that maybe I could work at La Curva. Have you been there, Father? I'm sorry, I didn't mean to ask you that. Well, you might have seen it from a distance. It's that little blue hotel with the red door, the one that's just where the road to Alvarado makes a sharp turn. Everyone knows it's a brothel but nobody talks about it. Well, I got a job there. I told my *comadre* Soledad that I'm working at the front desk of a hotel. It's half true, half false. I just don't want her to worry about me. Besides, she doesn't believe anything I say anymore. Why tell her the truth? If she wants to know it, she just needs to ask around the six hotels in town. But she won't bother to do it. Besides, I don't think I'm doing anything wrong.

"I change sheets and clean the bathrooms in the upstairs rooms. I have to wait for couples to come out so I can clean up, sometimes eight times in a single night. Some prostitutes work full shift. Others are part-time. And sometimes men bring their own from someplace else. I see them in their tight dresses, walking around on platform shoes, smelling of cheap perfume, chewing gum with their red lips open, and using words fit for a longshoreman working the docks. They seem to have developed a thick callus around their feelings. Survival. I wonder what is it they resent so much that their eyes lack shine.

"And those men, they look so wholesome walking around on the street. But you and I know the truth: I clean their sheets and then they come to you to clean their souls. I've had to change sheets stained with blood, semen, rum, piss. One blanket was so torn I had to make rags out of it. But no trace of Blanca. As much as I smell the pillows, I just can't identify her scent. And it's such an easy odor to spot. Fresh-sliced papaya with lime juice. Every time after she showered, the aroma floated around the house, tickled my nose, and a delightful sneeze made my entire being shake. I want to sneeze so badly, Father. I've been sleeping with a plate of red papaya on my night table and the smell has triggered in my dreams precise memories of my Blanquita. Practicing guitar on the portico, washing her hair in the kitchen sink, riding her bike to school. But I haven't sneezed at all. How can I? It's not her, in person.

"Father, I also want to confess on my daughter's behalf. I know she can't get to a church. Forgive her, I'm begging you. She must be in one of those filthy houses, pleasing men she will never see again. Butchers with huge bellies and lice in the hair on their backs. Truck drivers with disfigured souls and volcanoes of pus on their shoulders. Construction workers with the hands of reptiles that draw blood when they caress. Bureaucrats with innocent wives who know nothing. They must have her taking off her clothes ten times a day. Forgive her, Father. Forgive my daughter for all the sins they're making her commit. I'll do the penance for her. Do you want me to walk with Coca-Cola bottle caps in my shoes? Should I crawl on my knees across town, choosing cobblestone streets, praying one rosary after another before the eyes of my neighbors? Or maybe I should stick needles between my fingernails, wiggle them until I bleed, and dip the tips of my fingers in lime juice. I'll do anything you tell me to. I know you can't absolve through third-party confessions, but what have you got to lose? Just give her a temporary absolution until she can get to a church in person. That will give me some peace of mind."

Nobody knew who owned La Curva, but everyone knew where it was: along the sharpest curve between Tlacotalpan and Alvarado. People believed second-rate drug lords laundered money there. Some claimed it belonged to the state governor. Others assured, always under their breath, that La Curva was the headquarters of an anti-Catholic movement designed to keep priests busy listening to confessions and distracting them from the movement's ultimate goal: to create instability in the Church. Regardless, La Curva was one of the most visited places in town. More than the barbershop right before Easter, more than the best restaurant on Mother's Day, even more than the most popular ice cream shop in the middle of a weary summer day.

Mirrors everywhere reflected images of men and prostitutes dancing to the cadence of timeless boleros. Customers came in at different hours of the night to hire a whore, many times one they were already comfortable with and were able to call by her first name. Paintings of naked women hung on the walls, bright oil colors dabbed over black velvet. Officially, La Curva was supposed to be a bar, but the second floor had eighteen rooms for rent on an hourly basis. Patrons made their way up dark and anonymous stairs, hidden behind a large partition that led to the bar's restrooms as well. This way, no one knew who was heading where.

On her first day on the job, Esperanza had arrived early to cover the morning shift. Because she didn't want anyone to know where she was going, she got off the bus two hundred meters away and walked once the bus was out of sight. At that hour, only three men from Alvarado remained. Esperanza noticed them at the door. They were probably on their way home, their eyes sticky, their breath rancid and offensive. She imagined them greeting and hugging their wives and their wives asking, "Honey, how was your trip? Did you get a lot of work done? You look exhausted!"

Esperanza was sure she'd find a clue there, something that would eventually guide her to her daughter. San Judas Tadeo was not going to take her hand and walk her straight to where the girl was. Plenty of investigation on her own lay ahead. Luckily, she had watched detective movies since she was six. Her mother had started this tradition out of despair and loneliness, one year after her husband drowned in the flood. "Distraction takes the pain away," she'd tell Esperanza on the way to the movie house, back then the only building in town with air-conditioning. They'd always sit in the fifth row, right at the center, and Esperanza would guess who the bad guys were, what was going to happen next, and how the story would end with surprising accuracy.

She opened the windows of one of the brothel's rooms to let the sun come in. Her mother had taught her that sunlight kills bacteria, and there must have been germs by the millions trapped in La Curva. She shook the sheets. Dust particles flew up in the air, floating through the thin rays crossing the room.

After she made the bed with clean sheets, she inspected the soiled ones. They had lipstick stains. She bunched them up in her arms, sniffing them, desperately searching for a slight hint of papaya and lime juice. But the sheet only smelled of fermented fodder. On the night table, someone had left a set of dentures behind. Esperanza picked them up with the edge of her apron and put them in her pocket. She remembered seeing a lost-and-found basket downstairs, behind the bar, where customers could retrieve their belongings without having to ask anyone for them. She picked up the broom, the pail, rags, and Pine Sol. Then she put the dirty sheets in a canvas laundry bag and went to the next room.

Same procedure. She opened the curtains, the window, and pulled up the dirty sheets to inspect them. A cigarette burn. She passed her finger through the hole. She untied a pair of pantyhose from the headboard and, repulsed, threw them in a small trash can by the bed. At the bottom, she noticed a used condom. She had seen the packages featured in advertisements strategically posted in a concealed corner at the pharmacy and recognized the little black box with the golden word "Titán," tossed next to the soppy little rubber. She emptied the contents of the trash can into a bigger one that she wheeled around from room to room, but the condom had gotten stuck. She shook the can to release it, but that didn't work. She pounded the trash can bottom like a bottle of catsup. No luck. Finally, she removed it with the tip of the broom stick and got close to the window to get a better look. She had never seen one out of the package. She wondered if condoms were reusable. Luis never used those things. Perhaps she should put it in the lost-and-found basket.

On the third day of searching for clues, listening to patrons' conversations, and passing as a cleaning woman, Esperanza sat for coffee break with one of the prostitutes, Natasha, whose real name, Esperanza learned later, was Lupita.

"How did you get into this?" Esperanza asked.

"Why do you ask? Do you want to change jobs?"

"I was thinking about it. It's more money, right?"

"Yes. But instead of making beds, you mess them up. A stranger fucks you and tells you his most intimate secrets. Then you never see him again. Is it worth the money for you?"

"I don't know. Why do you do it?"

"It's not the money. It's revenge. My ex-husband thought he could fuck anyone. So I showed him that I could, too."

"Did he leave you?"

"No, I left him."

Natasha sipped her coffee. Esperanza dipped a piece of sweet bread in hers. Both women drank in silence. Esperanza wondered if passing as a prostitute would be a better way to know where Blanca might be. Men tell their secrets to prostitutes. Perhaps she could be one for a while. She could blend in. She could go from brothel to brothel and from oven to oven. It could be an option.

"I'm glad Fidencio is taping the soap opera episode for you, Father Salvador. I wouldn't want you to miss it, but I just had to come and see you. More so now that last night, I finally got a clue as to where I can find Blanca.

"I was downstairs in La Curva, putting away the brooms and rags in the utility closet. Some couples were dancing. A few drunken men and women walked around, rubbing their bodies against each other. The lights were dim. The atmosphere felt greasy and full of smoke. Two men walked into the bar talking and laughing, the taller one with a huge wart on his neck. I overheard their conversation. The tall guy said, 'I'm telling you, they've got girls, real kids. Thirteen, fourteen years old, no more. But you've got to book them in advance. And they don't give them to just anybody.'

"I had to find out where that place was but I didn't dare approach them. Then I saw a Heaven-sent little prayer card of San Martín de Porres pinned to the closet door. I touched him with the tip of my fingers as I said my prayer, pulled the card off the door and secured it inside my bra. I waited for the two men to order drinks. Finally, I screwed up my courage and asked the tall man, straight out, 'Excuse me, sir, where is that place you're talking about?' And he said, 'Oh, well, it's a secret,' and laughed at me, Father, but I couldn't afford to get mad.

The tall guy elbowed the short guy in the ribs and said to me, 'If you want I can tell you . . . in your ear.' He kept leaning toward me. I kept stepping back until a chair got in my way. I was scared, Father. Since Luis, no man has gotten so close to me. He must have sensed that, because he said, 'What's the matter? It's not polite to share secrets in front of other people? C'mon, let's go upstairs.' Then he told his friend, 'Wait for me, I need a ride home. It'll be just a minute.'

"I became certain that the man was confusing me with a you know what. He grabbed me by the arm and headed for the stairs. I couldn't panic, or else he would never tell me about this place, but the words came out in spite of me ordering them to stay inside my mouth. I had to say, 'Listen, I'm not what you think.' And then, without looking at me, he answered back, tightening his hand around my wrist until it hurt, 'Oh, no? So what the hell are you doin' here? Is this where you come to pray?' I didn't answer. We walked into room number 208. I had just cleaned it.

"He didn't waste time, taking his shirt off right away. I had to think fast. So I took a deep breath and jumped on the bed. Thank God that morning I had seen how a couple performed an acrobatic sexual encounter, more a show of fitness than sex, where the woman jumped right on the bed and yelling 'Catch me!' bounced back in the arms of the man, standing one meter away. I witnessed this completely by accident; don't think I'm spying on people or anything, I just happened to be cleaning the bathroom and they didn't see me watch the whole thing. Maybe they worked in a circus, I don't know. I thought of the delicate way Luis and I always made love. My skin had learned to read his fingerprints, his pore patterns, his hair follicles. I itched. I felt tickled. I shivered to his touch. One twinge after another. But we did not practice gymnastics. It never occurred to us. I wonder what other people do in bed that we don't know about.

"Just as the guy was unbuckling his belt, I yelled, 'Catch me!' and threw myself in his arms. He caught me, lost his balance, and both of us ended up on the floor. But that didn't stop him. He chuckled, 'Now I get it. You like to play.' I ran to hide in the bathroom. He chased me and cornered me in the shower, tearing my blouse off. As he pushed me around, San Martín de Porres' prayer card fell out of my bra. He picked it up, kissed it, and returned it to me, saying, 'So you do pray here, you little bitch!' He then pressed up against me. I was stranded between him and the shower tile. Father, I know my saints helped me on this one, because the man hadn't even unzipped his fly when he ejaculated prematurely, wetting his pants right around the zipper. Then he said, 'Fuck!' Now, I only say this word when I'm quoting someone, so don't count it as a sin, all right?

"Thank God that man was in a hurry. I know San Judas Tadeo gave me the strength to do what I did. The man dried his pants off with a towel as much as he could and looked at his watch. I got dressed quickly. My blouse was torn. He said, 'Shit, it's so late.' And I said, 'Well, it's not as if you wasted a whole lot of time with me.' Then I whispered, 'Thank God,' but he didn't hear that part. He answered, 'Shit. This always happens, no matter what, as much as I try to get more for my money.' He ended the phrase with a big burp that smelled of carnitas taco.

"I asked him about the whorehouse he had mentioned. He said, 'It's in Tijuana. Gringos go there and pay good dough to fuck teenage whores. It's known as the Pink Palace, but, hey, you wanna hear some good advice? Don't even bother going. You're one good-looking woman, don't get me wrong. I could wrap myself in that black mane of yours and sleep like a baby, if I had the time. But you're no teenager and they only take girls there. Besides, no offense, sweetie, but you're a little rusty.' He then gave me a tender pat on the cheek and handed me a fifty-peso bill. The hero printed on it had two little horns on his head, drawn with blue marker. The man left quickly, without saying good-bye. I put the money in my pocket and went back to my cleaning job, taking off the dirty sheets in room number 208.

"Can you believe it, Father? He gave me fifty pesos. Even with twice that money I couldn't get to Tijuana. Not even in a third-class bus, with smudged windows, more passengers than seats, and a broken muffler.

"And that's all I have to say. Please bear in mind that all these dirty words I've said were necessary for me to describe my sins. I normally don't talk like this. I'd better go. There are several men right behind me waiting for confession. They must be those men who have been coveting their neighbors' wives. I'm sure they'll keep you busy with their sins all morning. In the name of the Father and of the Son and of the Holy Ghost. Amen."

*   *   *

"I don't know, man . . . but every week it's the same story. How does he find out?"

"As far as I can remember, I've only coveted Mateo Salcedo's wife, but only in dreams. Now, the woman who was just in confession, she looks pretty darn good for a dream or two."

"How does this damn priest figure it out? It must be Fidencio. I'm sure he's the tattletale."

"Yeah, Fidencio's always watching us, but who knows, he's mute. How can he tell on us?"

"Sign language. I don't know. The Church has its ways."

"I wonder if we're all coveting our neighbors' wives all the time."

"The one I'd really like to get into bed with is Mrs. Martínez. Her children look so happy, she must have awfully sweet breasts. And she's not quite my neighbor."

"Man, don't you know that when Father Salvador says 'thy neighbor' he means every married woman, not just the ones who live next door?"

"He does?"

A third-class bus, with dirty windows, more passengers than seats, and a broken muffler, rode along the road to Tijuana. Esperanza had long ago left behind the palm trees and thick exuberance of Veracruz, and now tumbleweeds cavorted across the barren landscape of the Sonora desert, some of them rolling right in front of the bus, as if they had a death wish.

Esperanza rubbed off a grease smudge on the glass with her sleeve and prayed, ". . . and may San Rafael Arcángel accompany us so we arrive unharmed, body and soul. Amen."

She held the prayer card of San Rafael Arcángel, patron of all drivers and travelers. It was public knowledge that bus drivers always took their little San Rafael Arcángel's altars to get blessed after Mass and then they glued them to the dashboard in a ceremony that included heavy beer drinking. Then the drivers took their friends for a ride to prove that the bus and the driver were being looked after by San Rafael Arcángel, saving them from a drunk-driving accident. Esperanza noticed that the bus she rode on did not have a little altar of San Rafael Arcángel. Only decals of soccer teams pasted on the windshield. She held Blanca's photo in her other hand. How she'd hug her when she found her.

Across the aisle, a pregnant woman breast-fed a boy at least three years old who stood firmly on his little bare feet as if they had been nailed to the dusty floor. He was evidently experienced in traveling as a standing passenger. Esperanza wondered how many kilometers of land that little boy had seen in his short life. She hadn't really traveled much. The boy stared at Esperanza with eyes surrounded by too many eyelashes, like black tissue paper strands glued above the foil eyes of a piñata.

Sitting next to Esperanza was a young girl about Blanca's age. She licked a mango-on-a-stick sprinkled with chili powder. A comb hadn't touched her hair in weeks. Her clothes needed laundering and a few buttons were missing. On one foot, she wore a tennis shoe, no lace. On the other, a sandal with a torn strap. The girl idly leafed through a wrestling magazine, leaving her sticky finger-prints all over the pages. Did the girl even know how to read? One photo showed a huge, masked wrestler dressed as an angel, with a very impressive cape resembling feath-ered wings, cracking the back of another fierce-looking man dressed in tights. Esperanza felt a sudden need to touch that picture. The mesmerizing image of the winged wrestler made her forget to breathe and, after an entire minute, she remembered and gasped for air.

The girl licked a drop of mango juice off her arm. Esperanza reached for her purse on the floor and gave her a clean tissue. The girl took it without saying thank you. She watched the three-year-old boy sucking on his mother's breast.

"He's not a kid," said the girl to Esperanza, without taking her eyes off the boy. "He's a midget."

Esperanza heard the girl's voice for the first time and saw that under all that mess, she was pretty. She won-dered how an innocent girl could have such a twisted thought.

"What's your name?" asked Esperanza.

"Paloma."

"Are you by yourself?"

"Yeah."

"Where do you live?"

"In San Luis, in Monterrey, in Mexico City, in Guadalajara, I've even lived in Acapulco. When it's cold, I go where it's warm. When it rains, I go where it's dry."

The more Esperanza looked at Paloma, the more she looked like Blanca. Her chubby nose seemed thin, like Blanca's. Her snarled hair seemed silky and radiant, like Blanca's. Her dreary, little eyes seemed deep and full of meaning, like Blanca's.

"Why are you going to Tijuana?" asked Esperanza.

"Everyone goes to Tijuana sooner or later. I've been there twice."

"And your parents? Where are they?"

"Uuhh, they're fuckin' far." Paloma threw the licked-to-death mango seed out the window and, without asking, laid her head down on Esperanza's lap and fell asleep.

Esperanza felt an uncontrollable happiness as she experienced the growing warmth of Paloma's head on her thighs. Why not feel good about having met her? Paloma was homeless and had no relationship with her parents, wherever they might be. Perhaps she could come along with her. She stroked the girl's snarled hair. Esperanza looked at her daughter's picture once again. Then she picked up the wrestling magazine from the seat and looked for the winged wrestler's photo. Paloma was asleep. Her arm hung down loosely to the floor. Esperanza tore out the page, folded it, and quietly put it in her skirt pocket.

Esperanza and Paloma got off the bus at the Tijuana terminal. Paloma didn't have any luggage. Esperanza dragged her suitcase, the little wheels squeaking from lack of lubrication. She also carried a big cardboard box with the words "Fragile—Saints" scribbled on one side. The box was bulky and difficult to handle, but Esperanza hugged it close to her body as if she were carrying a child. Its contents rattled and clinked. It seemed to have a life of its own. Esperanza had heard on the bus that Tijuana was the most visited place on earth, mostly by people just passing through. By the worn-out tile on the terminal floor, she thought it might just be true. The dusty ceramic squares she was stepping on had long lost their pattern and gloss, and were worn unevenly, from the millions of feet that had walked on them in every direction, always on their way to somewhere else. According to a traveling pantyhose salesman who had sat a couple of seats behind Esperanza most of the way, Tijuana was the largest cantina in the world. He claimed he didn't remember anything that had happened during his previous trip. His hangover had lasted three days. The accountant next to him said that the whole city was just one huge whorehouse.

A man who hadn't spoken a word since he got on the bus heard the conversation and jumped into the aisle, big and menacing, right next to the other men.

"You don't know shit. I've lived in Tijuana for seventeen years and that's not what it's like," he belched. "Where else can you find a bilingual Santa Claus? Or a Chinese restaurant that serves sweet and sour pork tacos? And yes, it's one huge whorehouse, but size is not what counts. It's our women who make us famous."

To Esperanza, size did count. Perhaps it wouldn't be as easy to find the Pink Palace as she had first estimated. She had imagined Tijuana as a place with no owner, no law, no expectations or possibilities. But now that she was finally here, she just saw a city filled with people.

This isn't so bad, she thought, when a man, someone she could barely recall later, pushed her to the ground, grabbed her suitcase and the cardboard box, and ran toward the door. Paloma leaped behind him instinctively, catching up to him a few steps later and tripping him with her foot. He fell right in the middle of a group of Japanese businessmen. In the confusion, Paloma took the box from him, but the thief got up quickly and ran off with the suitcase.

"I fucked up. I could have snatched the suitcase, too," Paloma gasped.

Esperanza had not moved from where she fell.

"Don't worry, I didn't have many clothes. This box is what's really important. Thanks."

"Well, see you around. Maybe."

Esperanza watched the girl walk away, about to be lost in the crowd. Dragging her box, she chased her.

"Are you sure you'll be all right by yourself?" Esperanza reached for Paloma's arm.

"That's just what I'm wondering about you," said Paloma. "Your elbow is bleeding."

Esperanza hugged her. Paloma sunk her head between her breasts and stood still, accepting the caress. Esperanza noticed the girl had lice in her hair.

"I'll buy you lunch. How's that?"

A few blocks from the Tijuana bus terminal, Esperanza and Paloma walked by a four-table restaurant. Its walls were in urgent need of paint. The door was coming off its hinges and the menu jotted on a side column spelled tortillas with a "y," but the smell of home cooking lured them in. The incident with the thief hadn't diminished their appetites.

"I'll have half a chicken with salsa and rice with a fried egg on top, but don't overcook the yolk," ordered Paloma without looking at the menu. "And two quesadillas on corn tortillas. Oh, and a Coke."

Esperanza ordered just flan, expecting Paloma to leave some food on her plate that she could eat. Blanca never finished her meals.

"If you want, I can lick your scraped elbow," said Paloma with her mouth full of food. "You can't lick your own elbow. It's one of the few parts of the body where you need the help of someone else's tongue, or it won't heal."

"I'll be all right." Esperanza pressed the peeled skin with a tissue.

Esperanza wanted to comb the girl's hair, wash her up, buy her some new clothes and shoes, enroll her in school, kiss her, hug her, get her stickers with hearts and flowers, a brooch. She wondered what the girl's mother might be thinking at that moment, knowing that a daughter of hers was living on the street. She had to bite her lips not to ask Paloma about her parents. It seemed she didn't want to talk about them, or simply had forgotten who they were. Maybe she was better off living under parked trucks, eating out of garbage cans, washing car windshields at stoplights to make some money so she could buy a mango-on-a-stick for lunch.

Esperanza thought Paloma had ordered more than

she could possibly eat, but was pleased to see her nibble every piece of chicken nearly to the marrow. She ate her flan slowly and left a slice in case Paloma felt like having some.

The waiter, who was also the cook, added up the bill and put it on the table.

"No rush."

"Excuse me, I'm looking for the Pink Palace."

"It's a whorehouse, right?"

"I guess so." Esperanza hoped Paloma hadn't caught the word.

"Well, I've heard about it, but I don't know where it is. I've never met anyone who's actually been there. You should go and see a guy I know. I can't remember his real name, but just call him Cacomixtle."

"Cacomixtle? As in 'weasel'?"

"Exactly. He has a business like the one you're looking for. He might know."

The waiter wrote an address on a paper napkin and gave it to Esperanza, touching the palm of her hand with the tip of his fingers and looking at her with different eyes. Lewd eyes that she didn't know how to interpret. She had what she wanted. A lead. One step closer to Blanca. A little piece of hope on a paper napkin.

"Do you want some flan?"

Paloma said no and burped. Esperanza opened her wallet to pay and realized all her money was gone. She looked for it in every compartment of her purse, taking her things out and placing them on the table. Her comb. A rosary. Her sunglasses. A handkerchief. A mini–photo album with pictures of Luis, Soledad, her house, her cat Dominga, and several of Blanca. A pack of chewing gum. A key chain with the logo of Los Valerosos hardware store. An aspirin travel case. A ballpoint pen. Eight pocket-size laminated prayer cards of different saints, held together with a rubber band. But no money.

"I'm sorry. I lost my money." She looked frantically among her things spread out on the table.

The waiter sighed in search of patience.

"I'll take care of it," Paloma said. She pulled a bunch of bills out of her pocket and set one on the table like an accomplished poker player. "And I'm outta here." Then she disappeared into the street.

Just before the waiter took the money, Esperanza recognized the fifty-peso bill. It was the same bill that the man with the wart on his neck had given her at La Curva, the one showing a hero with horns painted with blue marker.

Esperanza sat there for half an hour until she understood how the fifty-peso bill had ended up in Paloma's hands and accepted that no girl would ever replace Blanca. How could she have ever compared her daughter with such a despicable little thief? Blanca had suffered from lice when she was six. That was the only similarity. Esperanza had to cut the girl's long raven black hair and treat her scalp with a solution so strong it dissolved a plastic comb before her eyes. And, like many children, she dreaded going in the bathtub, but once she was in, Esperanza found it impossible to get her out. It's true that she had not yet learned to be tidy. She was more like Soledad in that respect. Her things had a hard time finding their place in her room. But she was not a thief.

Now, deceived and with no money, Esperanza would have to look for the Pink Palace, find Blanca, and take her home to bathe.

Esperanza stopped in front of a motel with a huge blinking sign: EL ATOLLADERO MOTEL GARAGE. OPEN 24 HOURS. The word "Garage" was red and blinked faster than the rest of the blue sign. She crumpled the paper napkin with the address and put it back in her purse.

The door squeaked. The place was dim, smelled of damp carpet, and had a poorly stocked bar. At the edge, in the far corner, an old prostitute, her face hidden behind white strands of hair, drank tequila straight from the bottle with a man at least twenty years younger than she. Another man was busy at the back mirror, squeezing a pimple on his cheek. He had small, black eyes and a thin braid that went down all the way below his waist. Tattoos resembling snakes covered his arms. She closed the door slowly and set her cardboard box on the floor.

"Good evening. Excuse me, are you Cacomixtle?"

"People who like me call me that," he said, turning to Esperanza. "My mother calls me Liborio."

"Someone told me I could find out here where the Pink Palace is. Do you know?"

"Are you going to look for work there?" Cacomixtle inspected Esperanza. Her long black hair. Her legs. Her womanly silhouette against the light coming in through the open window, first red, then blue, as the motel sign outside blinked.

"Yes. Work."

"Do you have references? They don't just take any-one there, you know." His eyes were small and vulgar, yet seductive and powerful.

What kind of references would a prostitute give? This was an issue Esperanza hadn't considered.

"References? Oh, yes, I have eight years of experience with tall men, short men, fat men, blond men, old men."

Cacomixtle realized Esperanza knew nothing about the business. Still, he saw her as delicious prey. He imag-ined himself rubbing her body with perfumed unguents and then licking it clean again. Getting his tongue inside her ears, her belly button, her nostrils, her mouth, her vagina. Nothing had ever been denied to him. No one had ever stopped him from venturing into other people's orifices. Women from seventeen countries had felt the tip of his tongue causing an uncontrollable revolt inside them. They still remember, he thought, wherever they might be. He would not let Esperanza go. Why should he withhold his desire? Why should he repress his appetite before such a lavish banquet?

"Look, I think I can get you in the Pink Palace. A client of mine goes there regularly. He might come tonight. If you want, I'll find out for you."

"All right, then. I'll come back tomorrow."

With a big smile, Esperanza picked up her box and headed for the door.

"Do you have a place to stay?" Cacomixtle noticed the box.

"I'm going to look for a hotel."

As she said this, Esperanza remembered she had no money and imagined herself sleeping on a bench at the bus terminal.

"And what's this?" said Cacomixtle, looking around.

The room walls were painted red. The bedspread was mustard yellow. Nothing hung on the walls. Not even a landscape poster or a replica of any classic painting, like, say, *La Gioconda*. Only a big round mirror fixed to the ceiling, right above the bed. The intermittent light of the blinking motel neon sign came in through the twisted miniblinds covering the window. First, "El Atolladero" in red. Blink. Then, "Motel" in blue. Blink. Finally, "Garage" in red again. Blink. "Open 24 Hours." The sign went on and on, making a buzzing noise as it repeated itself over and over. Esperanza undressed and lay down. The bed was cold, the sheets vanilla yellow, uninviting.

Unable to relax, she rose again and reached for her box of saints. Esperanza began to set up a tiny altar on the night table with Blanca's picture, her late husband's, the picture of the wrestling angel torn from Paloma's magazine, the Virgen de Guadalupe, San Judas Tadeo, and a couple of candles that she carefully took from her box. Many more framed prayer cards, statuettes, crucifixes, and candles were wrapped in the sports section of a newspaper, but for now she only needed the basics.

"Luis, you have to understand," she said out loud to her husband's photo. "This is the only way I have to get our Blanquita back. I have no money. I know this is no place for me, but at least I'll sleep in a bed tonight."

The pillow smelled of rancid sweat. She threw it on the floor just as Cacomixtle opened the door.

"Is the client here?" she asked, surprised to see him.

Esperanza hoped she could get the address to the Pink Palace and leave this place.

"Not yet, but I brought you a little present."

Esperanza sat on the bed and bashfully covered herself with the blankets.

"If you're a whore, I'm the pope."

He handed her a tote bag.

"What makes you think I'm not?"

"Who do you think you're fooling? What do you want?" He noticed the little altar on the night table. "Let me guess. You need money to get to the other side and you think you're gonna get it working as a whore for a few days. Easy, right?"

"That's not it!"

"It's women like you who give the business a bad reputation. Wait till you come face-to-face with a naked stranger showing you his dangling hairy balls. You'll know that selling your body is like killing; sounds easy, but not many people dare to do it." And having said that, Cacomixtle left the room.

Esperanza was not selling her body. She was looking for Blanca. The selling and the killing didn't apply to her. But Cacomixtle didn't have to know what her intentions were. She locked the door this time and then sat down and opened the tote bag. Inside, she found a makeup kit and a carnation red spandex minidress with a very low neck and a much lower back. She smelled the dress. Sweet perfume. Talc. Deodorant. Someone had used it before her.

She sat in front of the mirror and turned on the switch. The lightbulbs around it lit up. Some were missing. Since she had all the elements, she decided to practice for her job interview at the Pink Palace. She imagined how she would look if she were to pass as a prostitute. Thick eyebrows. She widened them with a dark brown pencil. The left eyebrow seemed a bit higher, so she broadened the right one. Too much. She had to add to the left one again. Then the eye shadow. Electric blue with golden glitter sounded just right. Maybe a dab of fuchsia right along her eyelashes. Mascara. A lot. Like tarantula legs surrounding her eyes. And the lips. Red. Blood red. She had a hard time following her lip line, but she wanted to make her lips seem fuller anyway. The hair, distressed. As if someone had been pulling it. She didn't see any hair spray in the tote bag, so she teased her hair with her fingertips. When she was done, she stared at her image in the mirror. To her eye, she passed as a prostitute. The question was, "Is this the 'before sex' or the 'after sex' look?"

Trying not to ruin her hairdo, she carefully put on

the dress. A size too small, she thought. Her breasts wanted to spill out.

"Oh, dear Virgen de Guadalupe," she said to the stranger in the mirror, "I know that the road to Hell is paved with good intentions. Please help me!"

When she heard someone trying to open the door, she turned the mirror lights off, letting the neon sign's presence intrude in the room again. She hoped that Cacomixtle's client would just come in, volunteer the Pink Palace address, and leave without expecting anything in return. An innocent idea, she thought.

But no client was at the door. She heard a key turning in the lock and knew it was Cacomixtle.

"Mind if I come in?" he asked in a casual tone she was learning not to trust.

Esperanza quickly hid the makeup behind the tote bag and pulled a strand of hair in front of her face. She really didn't want this man to see her all dressed up.

"I see you're into costumes, baby." He was so close Esperanza could see the pores on his face.

"What do you want?" Esperanza was suddenly scared.

"If I had a fruit stand, I'd have to test my watermelon for ripeness before I sold it, don't you think?" His voice came through drenched in a sick kind of craving. The words floated off his wet tongue, which he set to work scouring Esperanza's ear. He thought he could easily develop a taste for her skin.

Cacomixtle rubbed against her so that she felt his erect penis under his pants. He ran his hands along her legs, her waist, her back. He licked her neck right under her ear and from there, like a snail, traced a thin road of saliva to the edge of her dress that barely hid her breasts.

"I've been addicted to tamarind candy since age four," he whispered.

She pulled up her shoulder straps, trying to cover her breasts. He unbuckled his belt. She looked at Luis' photo on the night table. He unzipped his pants. She prayed. He pulled down his briefs to his knees. Lit by the neon sign outside, their bodies became blue. Then red. Never in total darkness. Suddenly, just when his hands were sliding up underneath her dress, she managed to climb on the bed with an acrobatic ability she didn't know she had. Cacomixtle looked at her, amused and intrigued.

"Catch me!"

Esperanza jumped on him with all her strength, making him fall. He hit his head against the edge of the night table. The technique had proved successful before. It couldn't fail now.

"Fuck!"

Cacomixtle rolled over on the floor, his pants still at his knees. A gush of blood stained his forehead and dripped down over his right eye. Esperanza knew that even minor head injuries bleed copiously. She wasn't impressed. She took her shoe and pointed the high heel two centimeters away from his right eye.

"Don't you ever touch me again!" she warned.

He quietly dragged himself out of the room, not understanding how she could have rejected him. No one before had failed to succumb to his wet, slithery touch, to his manic passion. He knew, even before he was born, how to paralyze a woman, his saliva numbing the affected area, like a reptile's poison, only to attack his prey at will, expecting no resistance. He knew all he wanted was to satisfy his sucking and licking appetite, even when he was breast-fed by his mother. His taste buds were far too needy. And the tamarind-candy flavor emanating from Esperanza's skin made him feel a burst of desire unknown to him until then, a druglike rush. She was tougher than he had estimated and that made her even more appetizing.

Esperanza locked the door and pushed the dresser against it. Not that it would stop him from coming in again, but even these rickety forms of protection were better than none.

Before the sun rose, Esperanza had packed her street clothes in the tote bag, along with a wrinkled piece of paper she had found in the room where she had written a letter to Soledad at three in the morning. She crept down the stairs, all made up and wearing her costume. She had her box of saints in one arm and the tote bag and dirty sheets in the other.

Cacomixtle was sleeping on the lobby couch. He seemed as peaceful as someone who owes nothing. But as soon as Esperanza tiptoed past him, he opened one eye.

"Where do you want these? They're soiled." Esperanza handed him the sheets.

She hadn't found a hamper anywhere to drop them in and didn't see a cleaning woman on her way down to the lobby. She knew from her experience at La Curva that sheets should be changed even when used only once. They smelled of women's perfume, of rancid sweat, but not hers, since she'd hardly been in the bed, much less slept, afraid of Cacomixtle breaking in. Perhaps a prostitute had used the room before her.

"Come here. You're not scared of me, right?"

Esperanza cautiously moved closer to him. He took a pen from his shirt pocket, lifted Esperanza's dress, and wrote an address right on her thigh.

"The owner is Trini. Don't you say my name in front of her. Tell her Mr. Scott Haynes sent you. He's a client there."

"Thanks."

"Don't mention it." He rolled over on the couch to continue his nap, purposely showing lack of interest. Regardless of where he sent her, he knew she'd come back.

Esperanza picked up her box and headed for the door. Out of the corner of her eye, she saw the old prostitute from the previous evening holding a plastic glass with a picture of Miss Piggy and Kermit the Frog and in it her toothbrush and toothpaste. As soon as Esperanza left, the woman walked sluggishly over to Cacomixtle.

"You're fucked," she mumbled.

Cacomixtle grabbed her by her hair-dye-stained robe, sat her on his lap, and pulled her face close to his.

"Don't tell me you're jealous," he grunted.

"The devil loses when he falls in love."

"I'm not in love with her! She's just another little whore. Pitiful in bed. No potential. Looks are not the only thing that counts. That's why I sent her to Trini. You don't know shit."

"I know worse than shit. I know you. And just by looking at your eyes I can tell she's under your skin and won't get out until you shed."

"You're fucking jealous. That's what's happening."

"Now, that's a sick thought. In your whole life, none of your women has ever made me jealous."

"Not while you were one of them. But now that it's over, you can't deal with it. How many times have I said 'no more'? This is not a healthy mother-son relationship and I'm putting an end to it."

"You can't end what nature started."

"Why don't you go find a man you're not related to and snore by his side at another brothel? El Atolladero Motel Garage is mine. Or are you gonna take it away from me again?"

"I am not leaving. You are not leaving. This is our hotel. It's our creation."

"Yeah, but you gotta know when to quit. Hair dye's not gonna do the trick anymore."

"I thought you said looks are not the only thing that counts."

"In your case they are and they're gone."

"Fuck you!"

"You fuck you! What's more, go fuck Kermit the Frog!"

September 3rd (or is it the 4th already?)
Dear Soledad,

I am sure you already read my note. If you haven't, look for it under the iron that I left sitting on the ironing board. (I put it there so I could have a few days head start before you found it.) I didn't want to say good-bye in person because we'd still be hugging and wailing. But please don't worry about me. I'm in good company (I brought all my saints along) and even if you don't believe it, I can take care of myself. I've done pretty good so far.

I already made it to Tijuana looking for Blanca. I have concluded that she was kidnapped for child prostitution and is in a brothel somewhere in this city. This must be really hard for you to accept, but if you think about it, it's a better option than her being dead and gone. At least I can get her back. Imagining her in bed with strangers makes me feel the same nausea, only multiplied one thousand times, as the day that German tourist exposed himself to her last February. Remember we told her never to approach cars when asked for directions anymore? This is hard for me to accept, too, Soledad, but I won't stop until I find her, which is what San Judas Tadeo asked me to do.

Please make sure Dominga doesn't get out at night.
I don't want her having any more kittens. And don't
overwater my grandfather's hydrangea. Blanca and I
will come back soon. In my next letter, I'll be able to
give you a forwarding address.

I miss you,
Esperanza

P.S. By the time you get this letter you will probably be
enjoying the Independence Day parade. I imagine you
will be there, waving your little Mexican flag at the
children in their school uniforms, marching down the
streets and singing the national anthem. Did they do
the folkloric ballet this year? Did you make some of
their costumes? Now with Blanca and me gone, you
must have more time to think about yourself. You
never do that. You're always preoccupied with giving.
You've pampered Blanca so much. You've kept me
company all these years. Now you have all the
time you can think of in your apron pockets. What
will you do with it until we return? Spend it. Use it
to your advantage. You can't wait around for us.
Leave that to Dominga. By the way, did you give
Blanca's Jarocha costume to someone? I wonder.

The Pink Palace wasn't pink but blue. A corpulent man, his hair slicked back so that he looked like a sea lion sticking its head out of the water, opened the door just enough to get a quick glimpse of who was knocking. He held a red-eyed white rabbit in his arms.

"Good morning. I'm looking for Doña Trini."

Esperanza had already chewed off a couple of her fingernails before knocking.

"And who may I say is looking for her?"

"Esperanza. Mr. Scott Haynes sent me."

"The San Diego judge?"

"I guess so. He's a client of yours, right? He says that maybe I could work here."

"Come in."

The man looked down the street both ways before letting her in. Maybe she should have given him a fake name. Too late.

Esperanza followed the man down a hallway into a large living room with two closed doors on the back wall. Elegantly decorated, it seemed to her like the Silvia Pinal homes featured in the Mexican movies she remembered seeing in Orizaba, back in the early seventies: burgundy velvet furniture, two life-size marble French poodles standing on each side of the fireplace, gold-leaf wood tables with intricate carved designs next to a fiberglass chair resembling a hand inviting someone to sit on its palm, a glass case the size of an armoire filled with stylized porcelain ballerinas, paupers, and birds. On the sofas, plenty of pillows made out of all kinds of fabrics, textures, and colors. Crystal candy bowls. Purple shag carpets. A chandelier with at least one hundred lights, half of the lightbulbs missing. And just what Esperanza had expected to see in a fancy brothel: a replica of *La Gioconda*.

Doña Trini owned the Pink Palace. She was sitting by the back window in a wheelchair with an oxygen tank installed behind the seat. She wore a gray skirt, a pale peach V-neck cashmere sweater, and a pearl necklace. Her gray hair was up in a discreet bun. She could have been an ordinary grandma, but when Esperanza gave her a closer look, she couldn't tell if Doña Trini was a man or a woman. She could have been a grandpa dressed as a grandma, or a manly grandma.

"And who is this, César?" asked Doña Trini. Her tongue seemed to be too large for her mouth, and it got in the way of the words trying to escape through her teeth.

"She's Esperanza. *Mr. Haynes* sent her, Doña Trini."

"Ah. Bring us some tea."

Esperanza and Doña Trini chatted and drank chamomile tea like two ladies. They listened to a piece of classical music that Esperanza didn't even try to identify. Her ear was trained to boleros.

"This is not a brothel. It's not a one-night-stand motel or a whorehouse either. It's a private residence specializing in top-quality sexual services. And we only service people like Mr. Haynes."

César stood by the door holding his rabbit and listening to Doña Trini give Esperanza the Pink Palace's mission statement. It seemed to Esperanza that César must know this speech by heart, but still he stood there, attentive, offering the rabbit little pieces of carrot.

"Our clients are very demanding."

Trini sipped her tea, licking a drop that dripped down the outer side of the cup. Esperanza pretended not to notice.

"Did you bring an HIV test?" continued Doña Trini.

A jolt of anxiety attacked Esperanza when she heard the three dreaded letters. Blanca was now exposed to the disease and she, her mother, the one person in the world responsible for the girl's well-being, was not there to warn her about it. Esperanza had read about the horrors of the virus in magazines at the dentist's waiting room back in Tlacotalpan, but never told Blanca about it. Contracting the virus seemed such an unlikely event for her daughter. But it never occurred to her that the test would be a requirement to work as a prostitute. She had to answer quickly and it had to be believable.

"No, but Mr. Haynes had me take one last month and it came out negative."

"All right," said Doña Trini, tipping her head to look at a painting of a huge green wave, which hung tilted on the wall. "If you need anything else, I can have you see Dr. Oseguera. I send all my girls to him."

"Does this mean I'm hired?"

"On a trial basis."

Doña Trini had barely finished her sentence when she began to cough and hack. César hastily handed the rabbit to Esperanza and rushed to give Doña Trini the oxygen mask. She inhaled desperately while Esperanza tried to be friendly with the oversized animal. Within a couple of minutes, Doña Trini was back to normal, if that word could define her natural state. César grabbed his rabbit back.

"Esperanza is going to stay in Yuriria's room. That girl's not coming back," she instructed César in a raspy voice that made Esperanza instinctively want to clear her own throat.

Esperanza picked up her box of saints and her tote bag and followed César through a long corridor with several doors on each side. The thought that Blanca could be behind one of them made her want to open them, to call out her name, but she controlled herself. She had to go undercover, like a detective in a story.

Her room was the second to the last. The wallpaper was flocked, the large mirrors on each wall embraced by intricate golden frames. The bed had a golden column on each corner supporting a burgundy silk canopy. Each column was wrapped in a blown-glass grape vine. The crystal grape clusters matched the crystal grape chandelier on the ceiling. A picture of a nude woman embossed in gold over a purple background decorated the headboard. Esperanza sat on the bed and, to her surprise, it bounced. The mattress was filled with water. She had never been on mattress like this one before. César opened the curtains and rearranged some pillows on a chaise longue, oblivious to Esperanza's wonderment.

"This is your room and you can do whatever you want here, but it's got to be perfectly organized and tidy when a client comes in. Your monthly contribution is three thousand dollars."

"What?" she said, jumping up from the bed. "Three thousand?" For a moment Esperanza thought her whole plan had crumbled.

"Includes meals. Don't worry, you'll make much more. There are hangers in the closet."

César was turning to leave when Esperanza stopped him. All this was too much for her to take in on her own. She had to make immediate contact with San Judas Tadeo.

"And the kitchen? Is there an oven with a window?"

"Don't tell me you can cook, too!"

"I'm almost as good in the kitchen as I am in the bedroom! You'll see. One of these days I'll make you pork and beans."

"You savage!" said César. "That shit makes you fat."

"I can also cook carrot salad."

She gave César a closer look. He was clearly a man. She could tell by the bulk between his legs, outlined by his tight black pants. But she sensed a certain feminine side to him. It seemed as if he had stolen Doña Trini's femininity. Or maybe Doña Trini had stolen César's masculinity.

"And the other girls?" Esperanza couldn't waste any time.

"You'll meet them soon. If you need anything, ask me. Don't disturb Doña Trini. And one more thing, aside from clients, I'm the only man allowed in the Pink Palace."

Esperanza wasn't really listening to the house rules. She was looking at the textured picture of the nude woman over the headboard.

"Can I redecorate? A little?"

"Like I said, this is your room, but when you leave, you have to return it to me as it is now."

She noticed some dresses hanging in the closet.

"What about these clothes?"

"They're Yuriria's, but if they fit, they're yours, sweetie, except for this one." He grabbed a halter top made out of imitation leopard skin. "See you at one for lunch." César winked and closed the door behind him.

Esperanza sat on the water-filled bed, bouncing up and down. After she made sure César was gone, she pulled off the bedspread and sheets and with the palm of her hand kneaded the mattress. She put her ear to the bed and listened to the water gush inside.

"Oh, San Gerardo Mayela, patron of housewives, you've always been there for me. Don't think that because I'm surrounded by all this luxury I don't need you. Now is when I need you the most. And my dear San Pafnucio, you're the expert at finding lost, stolen, and misplaced things. As soon as my daughter and I reunite, I'll offer six Masses for you, at six in the morning, on the sixth month, just like my grandma taught me to do."

She lay on the bed as it undulated. She thought of Yuriria. Why was she not coming back? Had she been fired? Had she not passed the HIV test? Was she a minor, like Blanca? Had she escaped? Was she dead? How many girls were in Blanca's situation? How many mothers were looking for their daughters in brothels across the country? Too many questions to answer by herself.

She sat up and opened her box of saints, pulled out Blanca's picture, and touched it delicately with the tip of her fingers, as if she were transmitting life to it. She then pulled out a candle and a framed image of San Judas Tadeo. Then one of San Pafnucio, kneeling on a field with a human skull before him. She carefully placed everything on the night table. She lit the candle in a ritual she knew so well she could perform even when distracted with other thoughts.

"Dear San Judas Tadeo, I know you've been watching over me for many years. You've kept track of my good deeds as well as my stumbles. You were there when Luis touched my breast for the first time that night in the alley behind my house, one month before we got married. You stood by my bed in the delivery room when Blanca was born and with your breath helped her cry and fill her lungs with air. You protected me from the lightning strike that killed the mule standing by my side under the branches of an avocado tree during that awful storm that caught me in the fields. You saved me from getting my head blown off by the stray bullet that went out a bar window and hit the fuse box on the Mendozas' wall as I was walking by. Now I'm far from my home. But I know you're with me. I'm not a bit scared. I believe that when God made you a saint, back when you were killed by the heretics in Mesopotamia, He provided you with the divine ability to watch over a lot of people at once. If that's the case, please pay special attention to Blanca. Her guardian angel has always been very good at his job, but I'm sure he wouldn't mind a little back-up help at this difficult time in my daughter's life. Amen."

Two prostitutes were talking loudly and laughing in the bathroom. Esperanza opened the door a couple of centimeters, just to make sure she would not be intruding. The large mirrored space made it impossible to distinguish between the whores and their reflections. The scrawny one had a towel wrapped around her head and was washing her face with the precise and delicate movements of a facial expert. The dark-skinned woman was shaving her legs, raising one to rinse at the sink with the grace of a leaping frog. She had a tattoo of a palm tree along her thigh with a tiny monkey reaching for a coconut. The women were in their robes, exchanging bedroom gossip.

"I can take anything, but the pig pulled out a pitcher from under the bed and pissed into it right in front of me! He didn't even get up!" said the dark-skinned one.

"What, did he just turn over?"

The scrawny one leaned on the dresser and pantomimed a man rolling over in bed and relieving himself.

They both laughed hard, showing all their teeth, many with gold fillings. Esperanza hadn't heard anyone laugh like that in a long time. At least not while living with Soledad. These women were actually having fun, and she felt a sharp, sudden need to be included. Esperanza opened the door a bit more, just enough to stick her head in.

"Hey! You must be Esperanza," said the scrawny one.

"Yes. And you?"

"I'm Flaca. Trini said you come well recommended."

"No. Not really. A guy is just doing me a favor."

Esperanza found a tiny stool and sat. She was beginning to get tired of telling so many lies. She suddenly wished Flaca were her best friend and she could tell her the whole truth.

The dark-skinned one said, "I'm Morena. Where are you from?"

"Tlacotalpan, Veracruz. And you? Tijuana?"

"There are no natives here. Nobody belongs in Tijuana, honey," said Morena, pretending to be scared of the thought.

"But Tijuana belongs to everybody, so welcome!" Flaca said before she playfully splashed some water on Esperanza's face. The three women laughed so loudly that César, passing by with a tray holding two plates of salad, stuck his head in the bathroom.

"This isn't a boarding school dorm," he said bitterly, probably because he wasn't invited to join in the fun, thought Esperanza.

After he left, she asked, intrigued, "What's with the food?"

"Did you think he was bringing us room service? He eats it all!" said Flaca.

"And he never gains any weight, the fucking queer," said Morena. "Every day, he takes the same two plates to the Scarlet Room and brings them back empty. He must lick them clean."

"The Scarlet Room?"

"We're not allowed to go in."

Esperanza looked toward the door again. Two plates? A mysterious room? She was sure she was on the right track. So as to not create suspicion, she changed the subject.

"By the way, what's wrong with Doña Trini?"

"I don't know," said Flaca. "I think she got osteoporosis in her bones, from the menopause, I guess."

"Is she seeing a doctor?"

"Every Tuesday. César takes her. And she bathes in eighty liters of milk every Thursday."

"Maybe she should drink it instead," Esperanza said, sending her two new housemates into a fresh fit of laughter.

Tuesday is three days away, Esperanza thought. That would be the right time to look for Blanca in the Scarlet Room without getting caught, but if the opportunity came before then, she wouldn't wait.

Esperanza tiptoed into the kitchen. The house was quiet and the noon air was trapped inside, a stupor stalled within the space of every room, waiting for someone to open two windows so it could become a draft and escape. Some whores were napping. Three had gone shopping. Esperanza had seen Doña Trini wheel herself into the Scarlet Room and shut the door behind her. It was time for her to attempt contact with San Judas Tadeo. She softly whistled a tune, checking out the sacks of rice in the pantry, the sugar, a jar with black beans, detergent, soap bars. Suddenly, her eyes locked onto a can of Easy-Off. Horrified, she grabbed it with the tip of her fingers and sprayed every drop into the sink, as if it were cyanide. If anything could obstruct her communication with San Judas Tadeo, it was Easy-Off.

Once she disposed of the can and looked around to make sure she was by herself, she kneeled by the oven. The window is not as dirty as the one back home, she thought. But still, some large amber spots dripped down the glass.

She needed another apparition. She wanted to know what to do next. What if she sneaked in the Scarlet Room and found Blanca handcuffed to a bed? What if more girls were locked up? Would she help them all flee back home to their parents? Would they want to? Maybe their families had sold them. Or some doctor. What if she found that they were drugged? She had heard about that once. Perhaps there were no girls in the Pink Palace. Just Flaca and Morena and the other women, obviously already in their twenties. But then, what about the Scarlet Room? Who did Doña Trini keep there that no one else but César could see?

She tried to make her saint's image materialize. She moved to the right. Nothing. To the left. Nothing.

"Please! Don't leave me alone! Not now!" she prayed out loud.

After she pleaded, the silence grew to the point where she could hear the tiny flame of the stove's pilot flickering. The grease drippings on the glass did not take on any identifiable shape. Maybe her saint was busy appearing before someone else who needed him even more, or someone more important than she.

Esperanza didn't hear César walk into the kitchen, holding his rabbit. He watched her in silence for a while as she knelt in prayer before the stove.

"I've made it all the way out here. I've survived the worst. I hope it has been the worst. I never thought I would dare to do what I've done, and yet you don't give me a sign! How do you expect me to continue?" Just when she finished her prayer, she noticed César by the door.

"Is this woman strange?" he asked his rabbit. Then he kissed its whiskers and instructed Esperanza, "Go on to your room. Your client is here."

"Hello? Candelaria Church."

"Father! It's Esperanza!"

"Good Lord! Where are you?"

"In Tijuana, Father Salvador."

"That's what I was afraid of! Soledad got your letter. She came by. She wanted to know your address, but she couldn't get anything out of me."

"You don't know where to find me, do you?"

"Well, that's why she didn't get anything out of me. She was ready to go looking for you. I had to stop her."

"Thank you. I have so much to tell you, but I have to be fast before someone catches me on the phone. The owner of the house is taking a bath, so it's all right for a while. I'm staying at a house of sin, and it would seem odd to be caught making a long-distance call to a priest. The place is really fancy, but it's still a house of sin, even if Doña Trini doesn't think so. She's the owner."

"Esperanza, are you sure this is the right way to go about searching for your daughter? I'm already investigating the whereabouts of Dr. Ortiz on my end. You can look for her from here. You're taking too many risks."

"Oh, Father, I don't know why, but I just have the feeling I should do this. I am following San Judas Tadeo's orders. So much has happened. I need to confess."

"You know you can't confess over the phone."

"Father, nowadays the Pope flies all around the world on a plane. He undergoes surgery in state-of-the-art operating rooms with anesthesia and laser beams. He even rides in his popemobile. The Church is more modern than you think. Why can't I confess on the phone?"

"I'm sorry. Modernity hasn't made it to Tlacotalpan yet."

"For your peace of mind, how about if I consider this a confession, and you consider it a confidence?"

"All right. But just this one time!"

"As soon as I got to this place, the Pink Palace, I met an American. Mr. Scott Haynes, a huge man, blond hair, blue eyes behind thick glasses. A dewlap like a turkey's, an apron of skin over his neck. Strong hands but delicate fingers. He giggles when I talk. Someone told me to use his name to get into this house of sin. Father, if I pass as a woman of easy virtue, I can find Blanca faster. Sometimes men volunteer information to prostitutes. So, I told the people who run the Pink Palace that he had sent me and of course he found out.

"The first night he came up to my room, he said, 'So you're the one I supposedly recommended?' I was scared, Father. I could barely see his face because it was lit only by my candles. I said, 'Forgive me, Mr. Haynes. I really needed this job, and somebody gave me your name.' When he wanted to know who, I said, 'Yuriria. She let me have her room, Mr. Haynes.' I couldn't tell him about this man Cacomixtle, who's the one who really told me. I don't know what kind of relationship those two have. What if they hate each other? So, the Yuriria part is a lie. You may want to start writing down the sins, Father, or you'll forget them by the time I'm through."

"Esperanza, technically this is not a confession."

"Father, I need to be forgiven."

"You will, if you repent."

"I do, Father. Sort of."

"Well, there you have it. So, what happened next?"

"Then Mr. Haynes said, 'Call me Scott.' That's when I felt relief. I asked him if he was angry at me and he said, 'I won't know until I find out if I've made a good recommendation,' and having said this, he caressed my cheek. I just stood still. And when he was about to kiss me, he pinched me on my behind. I don't have to go into detail about what happened next with Mr. Haynes, Father."

"Please do. If it makes you feel better."

"This man has been good to me so far. He has come several times to visit now. I've seen him three nights already. On the third night, he gave me a fat roll of hundred-dollar bills and said, 'That's four thousand dollars there.' The two previous nights he had only given me two hundred dollars. I asked him why such an amount of money. He said, 'Do you need more?' Imagine that, Father."

"Did you get more?"

"No. I said I didn't need it. He wants me just for himself. I am lucky. I don't have to worry about other clients."

"I see. He bought your exclusivity."

"That's one way to put it. I don't know if that's common in this business."

"It happened in *The Truth About Giovanna*."

"Well, I never watched that soap opera, Father, so I wouldn't know. The other night I was in my room by myself. He had already left. It was daybreak. The sunlight from the window fell right on San Judas Tadeo's statuette, and I thought, 'What I'm doing must be a sin.' That's when I decided to call you."

"If you feel a need of repentance, then it's a sin. If not, it's not."

"He lies in bed by my side. We are always naked. He licks my breast. He says I remind him of his mother. I don't think that's a sin, but you tell me, Father."

"You haven't had sex with him?"

"No. I sing him lullabies from when Blanca was a baby. He has taught me others in English. He snuggles with me under the sheets and falls asleep."

"Is that all you do?"

"Yes."

"That doesn't sound so bad. When I was a boy my nana used to cuddle in bed with me and tell me stories."

"Father, this man is fifty years old. What if that nana of yours still snuggled in bed by your side?"

"Oh. She . . ."

"It seems sort of peculiar, don't you think?"

"Esperanza, my judgment of what is peculiar and what is not has been impaired since I met you. If this man is good to you, I'm at peace."

"So you agree it's not a sin?"

"I just wouldn't want you to get hurt."

"I'm fine, Father, but I haven't been able to make contact with San Judas Tadeo. Maybe he wants me to work on my own. I've been trying to look for Blanca in this house. From the outside it doesn't look as big as it really is. The hallway is long, almost like a hotel, one door after the other, all closed. That's where the prostitutes live. I have to say the 'p' word so you can understand me, Father. I don't mean to offend you. The women here are very nice. They even laugh and cry and worry about things. They may be hard on the outside, but underneath they're soft and sweet. I really don't blame men like Mr. Haynes. I can see why they like to come to this place. It's very elegant. Mr. Haynes says he has been coming here for years, crossing the border every other day, always looking for his mother. Well, not his real mother, but a woman who can make him feel loved and nurtured like his mother would have if she'd lived to watch him grow. He thinks Mexican women are more maternal. He says his father was very strict with him. That's why he became a judge. He says that, I don't know. So I spend some evenings with him. When he is not visiting me, I sit around with the other prostitutes. We comb each other's hair. We tell jokes. I've really come to like two of them, Flaca and Morena. They visit me in my room. They love my altar. Morena says it makes her think about God, but I don't believe it. She hasn't been to a church in years. We talk all night. The rest of the time, I look for clues.

"Last Tuesday, early morning, I walked around slowly, careful not to be seen. I listened for the voice of Blanca behind the closed doors. But I heard only silence. Most of the clients were gone. The women were asleep. Doña Trini's living room is at the end of the hallway. She was not there. César had taken her to the doctor. I saw them leave. He attached a big umbrella to the back of the wheelchair to protect Doña Trini from the nasty sun and walked toward the avenue. I knew I had some time to look for Blanca, but not a lot. Maybe one hour. I tried to listen behind the door of the Scarlet Room. I heard something like feet shuffling on the floor. I tried to open it but the door was locked. I have to go now, Father. I think Doña Trini is getting ready to come out of the bathroom."

"Call me soon."

"I will, Father, I promise."

Did you see how Esperanza put me on the spot, dear God? She didn't mean to. She knows nothing about what happened between Consuelo and me. An experience impossible for me to explain. And it wouldn't have mattered. What would I do if Consuelo cuddled in bed with me and told me stories now? I've thought about it all my life. I'd do the same thing I did that night before she left. But now I only imagine Esperanza. She comes in my room, stands by my bed, unbuttons her blouse, and I see she's wearing nothing underneath. She blows out all but one candle and in the darkness lies on top of me, just as Consuelo did, reaching for the most distant corners of my body. I unzip her skirt. I touch her skin. My fingers travel erratic trails up and down her shoulders, her back, her legs. She tells me stories about other men in my ear, like in the confessional box. Only now there is no screen to hide her identity. She tells me what she's done with the men she's met at the brothels. She shows me. I learn. I'm about to call her Consuelo, but I stop the name with the edge of my teeth and swallow it. We make love. I see myself as a young man again. The man I was just before I joined the seminary. Don't get me wrong, dear Lord. I don't regret having chosen to serve You. It's just that these thoughts pop up in my mind without my authorization, every night, after I say my prayers. By then You have probably left and are listening to other people. But I know You know. That's why I have never discussed this with other priests. Why go through them if I can tell You directly? I miss Esperanza. I want her back. I'm afraid she will not find Blanquita. Please watch over her. Amen.

Esperanza hung up the phone with Father Salvador and put her ear against the bathroom door. César and Doña Trini were still there.

"Don't move so much, you're making a mess. Like that, that's it. You have to rinse well or you'll get that rash again." She heard César's voice instructing Doña Trini in the bathroom.

"Try to get up as much as you can. I can't scrub your butt if you're sitting like that." César always had a difficult time bathing Doña Trini, but he did it every day.

"Get me the bedpan," ordered Doña Trini.

The Scarlet Room was the only place in the whole Pink Palace that Esperanza hadn't inspected. It was always locked. But, as Flaca had told her, the key hung from a pink ribbon on Doña Trini's dresser mirror. If Esperanza could get her hands on it, she could open the Scarlet Room and find out once and for all if Blanca was there. If she wasn't, Esperanza wouldn't waste more time. She would move on. There were hundreds of brothels still waiting to be inspected, thousands of prostitutes and pimps to talk to, millions of oven windows to stare at.

Esperanza heard the water from the shower shut off. She calculated she had a few minutes to find the key before they came out. Doña Trini's bedroom, the bathroom, and the Scarlet Room were only a few meters away from each other. She went into Doña Trini's bedroom quietly.

The dresser was a jungle of wigs, fixed with bobby pins on white Styrofoam heads, their eyes and mouth outlined with a ballpoint pen, probably by Doña Trini herself. Some were blond, some black. One was made into a French braid. Another featured a tall bun, the kind that was popular in the sixties. One, with no head to hold it, was all up in rollers. On one side, a silver tray filled with makeup, lipstick, and eyeliners. Numerous business cards were taped to the mirror. Lawyers. Dentists. Executives. All clients. Silk scarves of flamboyant colors and animal-skin patterns hung down over the mirror like snakes, obstructing any possible reflection. A hospital bed sat like a throne at the center of the room and, next to it, an oxygen tank, a TV set, and a table with a collection of snow domes inhabited by ballerinas, little gnomes looking out the windows of candy cottages, bunnies, and tiny Nordic towns in the middle of a winter landscape too foreign for Tijuana.

Before Esperanza could find the key amid the clutter, César came in the room wheeling Doña Trini, who wore a silk robe and had a towel wrapped around her head.

Without makeup and with glistening skin that appeared to be freshly shaved, it seemed to Esperanza Doña Trini's face could pass for a mackerel's. An old male mackerel, if such gender distinction could be made. She wondered, not for the first time, if maybe Doña Trini was indeed a man.

All three of them were shocked at the encounter. César rolled up his soaking wet shirtsleeves in nervous little jerks.

"Did you lose something?" Doña Trini was blunt.

"You. I lost you. I was looking for you. I'd like to know what Mr. Haynes thinks about my work." Esperanza answered fast, without even thinking of a good excuse to be in Doña Trini's private quarters.

"He adores you," said Doña Trini in a softer tone.

"I think he likes the candor of the girls from Tlacotalpan." Esperanza gave Doña Trini her most sincere smile and calmly headed for the door, her insides a riot of nerves.

"By the way, Esperanza, you are only allowed to be in your room and the common areas of the house. Didn't César tell you?"

"Yes, Doña Trini."

Esperanza left the room wondering what kind of consequences she was supposed to expect.

"Why are you so easy on Esperanza, may I ask? If you had caught anyone else in your room, you would have made me fire her on the spot."

"I don't know. I like her. I guess her long fingers remind me of my aunt Concepción's."

"Was that your aunt burned alive by the revolution-aries?"

"No. That was Encarnación. Concepción was the one who survived. She saved me. We hid in the shed. They took all the cows except for one with a broken leg. I named her Felícitas the First. The famous Felícitas the First. She had a baby calf. I named her Felícitas the Second. My milk sister. We learned everything there is to know about life together."

"How old were you when the attack happened?"

"You're not going to trick me into telling my age, you smart ass. But to give you an idea, two months later, my aunt took me into town in a basket and had me baptized by the name of Trinidad. But I've always gone by Trini."

"Was she your godmother?"

"Yes. Everyone else was killed by the soldiers. My mother was raped first. The ranch was burned to the ground. The revolution had already ended six months before, but that particular regiment had not been informed. I grew up sleeping in the shed between my aunt and the cows. Why do I have to tell you the same story every other week as if you've never heard it before?"

"I know, I'm terrible. I shouldn't do this to you, but I love it when you get melancholy. It makes me want to rub my groin."

In the days that followed, Esperanza set up a full-blown altar in her room. Scott Haynes had gone to Europe on vacation with his wife, so she found more time to devote to her search.

Statuettes of San Judas Tadeo, San Ramón Nonato, San Pascual Bailón, San Pafnucio, and San Martín de Porres were lit by novena candles featuring decals of the same saints, and around them three glass vases with red carnations, all carefully arranged on the chaise lounge, the larger saints in the back, the smaller ones in front. A beautiful glow-in-the-dark San Miguel Arcángel. A Virgen de Guadalupe surrounded by dusty silk roses and illuminated by a pink lightbulb. A Sacred Heart with a receptacle for holy water. A crucifix mobile dangling over the entire altar. Pictures of more saints pinned to the wallpaper. And, of course, Blanca's photo right next to the statuette of San Judas Tadeo, whose tiny tongue of fire lit up by itself in the evening thanks to a minilight sensor discreetly placed at the back of his neck.

She also kept a pad on her night table where she had written prayers with alternative outcomes to her ordeal for the retablo she was planning to paint on a sheet of tin, as was customary, and offer to San Judas Tadeo at his famous shrine in Mexico City when she found Blanca. The prayer options read as follows:

Option 1: "Esperanza and Blanca Díaz give infinite thanks to San Judas Tadeo for helping us come together again in good health after a horrible incident in which the child Blanca was kidnapped and sold by a doctor and held against her will as a girl of easy virtue. The misfortune happened to Esperanza and Blanca Díaz last August. After a frightful search throughout the country of Mexico, ending up in the faraway city of Tijuana, the girl was rescued by her own mother from a secret Scarlet Room along with other girls, victims of the same torment. In thanksgiving for this evident miracle, we post this retablo on the walls of the San Juditas temple."

Option 2: "I make this miracle public. My twelve-year-old daughter, Blanca, was taken away from me by an evil doctor last August after a simple surgery from which she came out well, but from which the doctor said she had died. San Judas Tadeo appeared before me and asked me to find her. Because the authorities were incapable of helping me, I had to invoke my saint with true heart and look for her on my own, finally finding her with the miraculous and timely guidance of my saint. With the invaluable help of a good-hearted American man, she managed to escape with other girls from the Pink Palace. I entrusted her safe return to San Judas Tadeo, and today we are together thanks to him. Esperanza Díaz. Tlacotalpan, Veracruz."

Esperanza didn't know if there were indeed other girls, or if Scott would help her. She didn't even know if Blanca was in the Pink Palace at all. But she'd write the real ending to her search as soon as she found Blanca and took her back home. She would have to get a sheet of tin and some paint to illustrate the scene of the very moment when she was notified that her daughter was dead and she couldn't see the body. Or perhaps she'd depict the scene at the morgue where she grabbed the doctor by his coat and pushed him, and Soledad and the nurse had to pull her away.

She remembered her own mother painting a retablo for the Virgen de la Candelaria. Featured in it was Esperanza as a little girl with her mother up on the church bell tower, both screaming for help, the streets flooded, rain pouring, and down the river, her drowned father lying next to a dead bull. Esperanza had prayed many times in front of that retablo, still nailed to the wall in church. She knew the inscription by heart:

"My Mother, my dear Virgen de la Candelaria, I give you eternal thanks for the miracle that you granted us, saving me and my daughter from drowning by guiding us up to the bell tower of your church during the flood where my husband, Refugio, lost his life, being dragged along by the waters of the Papaloapan River and being found drowned by the river bank. I thank you for saving the rest of my family, my child Esperancita. In gratitude, I offer you this retablo. Socorro Díaz, Tlacotalpan, Veracruz."

"Sometimes saints and virgins perform miracles without us knowing," Esperanza's mother had said, teaching her daughter to be grateful for every miracle. So, when Esperanza fell off her bicycle and only injured her left knee, she thanked San Rafael Arcángel, patron of the roads, and glued his tiny statue to the steering wheel of her bike. When she successfully prepared the complicated stuffed-crabs recipe for her wedding meal, she thanked San Pascual Bailón, patron of cooks and housewives, and set up an offering in the kitchen that included garlic cloves, sliced onions, and twelve different types of peppers. When her cat got hit by a car and survived, she thanked San Francisco de Asís, patron of animals and pets, and took his statue (and the cat) to be blessed. When she found the locket Luis had given her on their first anniversary, she thanked San Pafnucio, patron of lost people and things. Now she would have to pray to Santa Artelia, patron of kidnapping victims.

"God can really do it all single-handedly, but He's the boss, He can afford to have as many assistants as He wants," Esperanza often told Blanca.

And continuing the tradition, Esperanza taught Blanca to invoke her saints whenever she needed them and thank them as well for everything good that happened to her.

So, as she knelt before her altar in her room in the Pink Palace, she called on her saints. "My *santitos,* all my beloved little saints, I'm sure Blanca is now praying for her well-being as much as I am. You've always been so good to us. Now that we're in real trouble, I know you won't disappoint us."

Esperanza turned to Santo Niño de Atocha, with his little brimmed Spanish hat bearing the Compostela shield, his spears of wheat, and a pair of shackles on his left hand and his basket of withered silk wildflowers on the right. He was peacefully sitting on a miniature bindweed chair. While living at Esperanza's house, he had stoically accumulated dust as he sat for six years on the top shelf of the china case in the dining room, next to Soledad's porcelain bird collection. But now that he was on the road with Esperanza, it seemed to her that the flowers had recovered some of their vitality and even his cheeks were a bit rosy.

"Santo Niño de Atocha, you rescue us from danger and violence, so you must know by now what's going on: Blanquita is in a very dangerous situation and needs your help. I don't know how close or how far I am from her. She may be a few steps or thousands of kilometers away. So while I look for her, whether she is in this big house or somewhere else, please take care of her. I always pray to you for the victims of drug lords, but this time I am praying for my daughter, with all my strength."

Esperanza touched the velvet robe and made the sign of the cross. The wildflowers in Santo Niño de Atocha's basket were moist and their petals covered with dew. It was time to visit the oven again, as she had done every morning for the past two weeks, while everyone slept. She stepped out of her room, making sure no one watched her.

Doña Trini walked slowly down the hallway, exercising her legs by rolling her walker along the shag carpet. She did this every day with a great deal of difficulty, her unstable steps making the rest of her body wobble.

"Doctor's orders are doctor's orders," she'd mumble as she pushed the walker.

The effort seemed more than she could handle, but her arms were strong and not many obstacles could really keep her from where she wanted to go in the one-story house, except for a couple of steps at the end of the hallway, right at the entrance to the living room. Esperanza had heard her ask César to call the carpenter and have a ramp made. She complained that the bumping and banging of the wheelchair going up and down those steps was beginning to affect her spine.

Doña Trini had just taken her milk bath, as she did every Thursday. Esperanza wondered how she was able to get enough fresh milk to fill a bathtub in a city where it was often scarce. Maybe a client of hers owned a dairy. Maybe she was friends with the milkman.

Esperanza followed her in silence, at a distance. She saw César in the living room, holding a bucket of alfalfa. He was talking to a stranger. When Doña Trini went in, they greeted her. They laughed politely. They whispered something. Esperanza couldn't hear but she could get a good look. The man wore a dark blue suit, white shirt, and a Mickey Mouse tie. He was probably an American, a new client. She was glad she only had to deal with Mr. Haynes, but the idea of that man touching Blanca disturbed her and she preferred not to even think about it. She managed to sneak into the kitchen.

She sat on the floor in front of the oven window. She opened the door, looked inside, and then closed it again. She looked at the glass from different angles as she always did, she scratched a little bit of grime with her fingernail, but no saint.

Flaca appeared, still in her nightgown, to heat water for coffee and found Esperanza by the stove.

"What the hell are you doing sitting there?"

"Just wondering what I'm going to cook next. It's inspiring to sit like this."

"I'll try it sometime. Come on, I'll cut your hair." Flaca had worked as a hairdresser. Though Esperanza would have preferred a visit with a saint to one with a whore, she followed Flaca back to her room, vowing to return to the oven the next morning.

As Flaca clipped away, Esperanza felt weightless for the first time in thirteen years. She hadn't cut her hair since Luis was killed in homage to him. Her hair had been the one feature he adored the most. But he was dead. Now she looked in the mirror and she didn't see a widow anymore. Flaca had cut her waist-long black hair to her shoulders and parted it down the right side instead of in the middle. Esperanza rediscovered her neck, longer than she had thought. She pulled a tube of foundation from Flaca's makeup kit and applied it. Then eye shadow, eyeliner, blush, lipstick. She had been practicing, and it showed.

The image reflected in the mirror was of a woman Esperanza didn't know existed, or could. A fragile glow on her face made her look vaporous and airy. Was the mirror smudged? She wiped it with a cotton ball, but the image she saw still reflected a gentle radiance, an intangible light. She took the braid of black hair Flaca had cut off, tied a red ribbon around it, and brought it back to the altar in her room.

"Dear Virgen de Guadalupe, here is my braid. It's for you. I'm sure you've had tons, truckloads of hair offered to you since you first appeared before Juan Diego. Millions of women must have already offered you their braids. But this has been a part of me since Blanca was born. It means a lot to me. Please, help me find my daughter. I'm begging you."

Scott Haynes came back from Europe and brought six envelopes full of pictures to show Esperanza. After complimenting her on her new hairstyle, they sat on the bed to look at the photos.

"This is Gladys, my wife."

He pointed at a small yellow dot in a mountainous landscape somewhere in Switzerland. In the next picture, the yellow dot was now a tiny person standing in front of a spectacular fountain in Italy. In the next picture, the woman was wearing a baseball cap and dark glasses. And in the next picture, this one taken in a painstakingly groomed garden in France, Esperanza saw that a few strands of her blondish-gray hair had snaked out from under the cap. In the last picture, Esperanza noticed that the woman looked neglected and lonely. She didn't smile. The dark glasses she wore in every photograph hid the color of her eyes.

"I'm leaving Gladys," he said as they looked at the last photo. "Will you move in with me?"

"Unfortunately I can't." Esperanza answered. "You know I have to find my daughter."

Scott rubbed his dewlap. Obviously he wasn't expecting such an answer, especially not delivered in such a straightforward way.

Before his trip, Esperanza had shown him Blanca's picture without confiding to him why she was looking for her in brothels, of all places. But now that he had dared to show her his wife's photos, she felt a sense of trust.

"She was kidnapped for child prostitution."

"How can you be sure?"

Esperanza told him about San Judas Tadeo's apparition.

"Do you know all this for a fact?" he insisted. "You don't have sufficient evidence to prove that she is not buried in the grave."

"She is not. The coffin was empty. I heard it echo. And please, Mr. Haynes, you are not in court. Don't try to find evidence. I have divine orders and I must follow them."

He understood that nothing more was to be discussed and, to end the conversation, he embraced her.

"Call me Scott."

The notes of a bolero came through the window from the next room. Scott began to rock Esperanza in a very slow dance. She whispered dainty nothings in his ear, like a mother. A single light came from the altar, which had more than doubled in size since he left. More saints, more flowers, more candles. More reverence. After they danced for a while, he dragged a screen from where it lay folded against the wall and, as he always did, spread it open in front of the altar. Once the saints were out of sight, he felt it was polite to take his shirt off. Esperanza undressed and he cuddled in her arms. They talked for three hours, side by side on the water bed.

"You wasted twenty-six years with a woman you don't love. I've missed my husband for thirteen years." This was an unusual sensation for Esperanza. She found herself communicating better with a stranger—even in her broken English—than with Soledad.

The following night, Scott showed up again with a present for Esperanza. She unwrapped the box carefully, so as not to tear the paper. She hadn't received a gift in a long time. A pair of shoes. Daring, high-heeled shoes. She hugged him and tried them on. The red straps glowed against her slender dark ankles. She promised herself to keep them for as long as she could, no matter how many new heels and soles they'd need.

Scott went back to Gladys in San Diego to ask for a divorce. Esperanza walked along the hallway to Flaca's room, wearing her new shoes. Morning light came through the windows, promising a day without clouds. Out of the corner of her eye, she saw César standing outside the Scarlet Room like a professional bodyguard. He checked his watch and returned to his pose.

Esperanza knocked. Flaca took a couple of minutes to open. Her hair was snarled. She had a false eyelash stuck to her blush-smeared cheek. For a second Esperanza thought it was a spider and was about to swat it when she recognized what it was and stopped her hand midair. Flaca didn't even blink. She had been drinking and the smell of alcohol rose from her skin, mixed with Sanborn's cologne, sweat, and someone else's breath.

"I have to sleep some more. I'm beat. Can you come back in three years?"

"Why don't you come over later? I need to talk to you."

It took Flaca all morning to get to Esperanza's room. She liked the altar, but it disturbed her. She grabbed San Martín Caballero riding his horse and took a peek under his robe. Esperanza snatched the statue from her hands and put it back, respectfully.

"If you want your business to thrive, you pray to him," said Esperanza.

Flaca was sure Esperanza had set up the altar as a kind of decoration to excite her client. No religious purpose at all.

"So?" asked Flaca.

"I have to know what's going on in the Scarlet Room."

"What for?"

"I don't know. I'm curious."

"Doña Trini doesn't let us in, and you know what? I don't care. It's her own twisted little hobby."

To the women's surprise, Doña Trini opened the door in the middle of their conversation.

"Esperanza, see me in my room in one hour, after my therapy."

"Yes, Doña Trini."

She didn't slam the door when she left, but Esperanza still sensed that Doña Trini was upset.

"Do you think she heard us?" she asked Flaca.

"No, don't worry. She's been losing her hearing for years." But Flaca looked concerned.

Though Flaca passed the time with her, it became a very long hour for Esperanza, almost as long as the hour she spent in the morgue waiting for Dr. Ortiz to give her permission to see Blanca's body.

"Who's the youngest whore you've ever met?" asked Esperanza out of the blue.

"As in 'underage'? Maybe I have met someone, but I wouldn't know. Everyone does their math. If you're under eighteen, you add. If you're over thirty, you subtract."

Aside from Flaca and Morena, Esperanza hadn't really befriended any of the other prostitutes, but she'd asked all of them questions in search of leads, with no luck.

The hour was up and Esperanza walked down the hall to find Doña Trini's door half shut. Through the opening, Esperanza could see a strong male arm bending a hairy leg back and forth, back and forth.

She knocked and heard Doña Trini say, "It must be the girl."

Esperanza waited patiently. Finally, Doña Trini said a little louder, "Come in."

The woman lay on her stomach. She was on a collapsible massage table covered by a thick cow hide. César was finishing the therapy. The lights were dim. The room was full of heavy fabrics: bedspread, drapes, rugs, towels. All pink. The air felt a bit stuffy. The smell of Ben-Gay ointment reached Esperanza's nose and made it itch. César pulled down Doña Trini's nightgown to cover her hairy legs and helped her sit in her wheelchair next to the table with the snow-dome collection. She covered her shoulders with a pink knit shawl.

"I'm going to be very straight with you. The word is out about your altar, and my other clients want you. I need you to take care of them. Otherwise they're just going to go somewhere else."

"But Mr. Haynes has asked me not to see anyone else."

"I know. But he doesn't have to find out."

"But if he does, *he'll* go somewhere else."

"Look, I've already lost two clients because of this exclusivity shit."

Esperanza thought quickly. If she was forced to see other clients, like that American in the Mickey Mouse tie, she'd no doubt have to commit all sorts of new sins. Father Salvador would surely be disturbed by such a confession. Then an idea came to her.

"I'm sorry, Doña Trini, but lying to Mr. Haynes will not solve anything. I don't know why you're losing customers, but maybe what this house needs is a spiritual clean-up, like we do back home."

Doña Trini hadn't considered the possibility of the house being under a bad spell. She looked at César, puzzled.

"There's a lot of witchcraft going around. Who knows, you may have an enemy using it against your house." Esperanza was certain that Doña Trini had at least one enemy she could think of.

"I can think of eight enemies already," snapped Doña Trini, as if she were reading Esperanza's mind.

*   *   *

A barbecue grill with red-hot charcoal let out enough smoke to stain the wall with a tongue-shaped plume of black smut. Burning branches of special herbs and plants released an assortment of smells that mingled in the air, causing some of the prostitutes to sneeze. Esperanza had lined up all twelve women, naked along the wall, as well as César.

Esperanza helped Doña Trini undress for the spiritual clean-up, but the old woman refused to take off her bra and panties. She sat in her wheelchair at the end of the line, right next to Morena, who was severely bruised. Some clients were rough. Esperanza had heard her crying two nights earlier, after the beating she took from an aerospace engineer who normally showed up drunk.

"It's very important that the smoke gets to every one of the rooms in the house. Every single one." Esperanza noticed that Doña Trini looked a bit nervous.

The ritual began. Esperanza had never conducted one before but had undergone so many in her childhood that she knew exactly what to do. Her grandmother would take her at least three or four times a year to visit Don Sabás. He minimized her allergies by making her drink a yarrow and slippery elm concoction with a few drops of squirrel's urine. Not only was he a well-known shaman for his ability to extract bad spirits from people but a very good *curandero*, too. Even doctors went to see him with an array of ailments: lumps under the skin, which disappeared at his touch; diarrhea or constipation, both cured by the same herbs; insomnia, which his hyssop and catnip potions helped dissipate; flatulence completely eliminated by his wild yam and fennel tea.

For toothaches, echinacea and rabbit-liver ointment. For painful joints, black cohosh and celery seed compresses. For hair loss, devil's claw and two drops of menstrual blood in a chickweed lotion. For bad breath, agrimony and red clover infusion. As a sex enhancer for women, damiana tea. For men, the Indian herb ashwagandha. For impotence, skullcap, licorice, dandelion, and lots of prayer.

Tlacotalpan was a short drive from Catemaco, home of Don Sabás and capital of witchcraft country. People from the entire republic went there to cure their ailments, to get an enemy killed, to contact a dead relative, or to have their futures told. Don Sabás was a master in medicinal arts, but he died tragically after he transformed his body into a ball of fire to fight against a feared rival. He ate the wrong fungus and could not return to his natural state. Becoming a pile of ashes, he was swept into a dustpan and sprinkled all over town, as he'd instructed his niece in a dream. Fortunately, Esperanza's allergies diminished with time, and she no longer required his services.

Esperanza didn't expect to rid the house of the spirits, or Doña Trini of her bad breath. That required a special gift she didn't have. But at least she'd go through with the ritual to find out who was locked up in the Scarlet Room.

First she gave everyone a cup of tea made with three different kinds of herbs. She had gone to get them at the market the previous day, from a local *curandero* recommended to her by a door-to-door shoe repairman who fixed the heel of one of her shoes. Then she took a leafy eucalyptus branch from the grill and fanned it on each whore, hitting them gently all over their bodies. Some giggled at the sight of the lit smut flying off the branch and falling dangerously on the shag carpet, which fortunately did not ignite. Others took the clean-up as seriously as surgery. Especially Morena, who, no matter how much perfume she dabbed behind her ears, on her wrists, between her legs, or on her nipples, smelled of paint thinner. As a little girl, her skin had become impregnated with the smell when her father, a painter, would come home at night after work and caress her, maybe a bit too much, without washing his hands.

As Esperanza finished with each prostitute, she sent her to bed. Each had to lie down for one hour, until her wounds healed. Casimira had been in love with her folk-loric ballet teacher, who later jumped off a cliff with another lover. La Mojadita had been given away by her grandfather at age six to an old aunt who made her sell Kleenex and chewing gum to motorists on the street in order to pay for her room and board. Flaca had killed the man she loved, entirely by accident. While getting ready to go out one Friday night (before she became a whore), she inadvertently dropped her hair dryer in the bathtub where her man was soaking peacefully. He had just made love to her like no one ever would again. Everyone had a wound to heal.

With great veneration, Esperanza took an egg and rolled it over Doña Trini's entire body. She then broke it into a glass of water and made a big show of analyzing the yolk and the white.

"No wonder, Doña Trini. Somebody did a little job on you."

"That must have been Cacomixtle," said Doña Trini. César nodded.

Esperanza pretended not to recognize the name. It didn't surprise her to learn that Cacomixtle was at the top of Doña Trini's enemies list.

"But it's out now. The evil. See? Here it is." She pointed to a white scum inside the glass.

Doña Trini watched the gooey floating spitlike mucus with disgust and collapsed in her wheelchair, relieved that the evil was officially out.

Then, to rid the house from any leftover bad spirits, Esperanza fanned the eucalyptus branches in the hallway and then entered each one of the rooms, filling them with a dense smoke. The prostitutes obediently stayed in their beds, nauseous from the lack of oxygen. When Esperanza reached Doña Trini's room, she helped her get dressed.

"Now I need you to open the locked door. I have to eliminate every spell that they may have cast on the property."

Once at the door of the Scarlet Room, Doña Trini pulled the key with the pink ribbon out of her bra.

"You must swear that you'll keep this to yourself," she said.

She made sure no one else was around and opened the door. Inside, a strong and beautiful Holstein cow, standing peacefully in the middle of the room, turned to stare at her. The walls had red velvet tapestries. Fancy brocade and lace pillows lay all over the floor, a chaise lounge was placed on one side, and a crystal chandelier hung from the ceiling. A wooden ramp large enough to elevate the wheelchair a couple of feet was pushed into a corner. The cow looked at Esperanza with her big, expressive eyes framed by lush, feminine eyelashes. Speechless, Esperanza turned to Doña Trini, hoping to get some sort of explanation. But Doña Trini only admired her cow, tenderly watching her chew the cud.

"Meet Felícitas, the Sixth."

"Hello, Felícitas."

"You can call her Feli," said Doña Trini.

Esperanza went around the room, mechanically fanning her branches and avoiding stepping on the cow dung.

"Not a word of this to anyone, Esperanza. She is not to be shared."

"Yes, Doña Trini," answered Esperanza, about to cry.

No locked-up girls. No Blanca.

Esperanza burst into the kitchen, demanding answers of her saint. She grabbed the oven door and slammed it again and again.

"There are no girls locked up here! You're not helping me find Blanca!"

She was wrathful, sick, deceived.

"Is this the kind of support I'm supposed to expect?"

She kept on slamming the oven door violently until the door fell to the tile floor and the little window shattered. Tiny glass slivers spread like uncooked rice all over the floor, reaching under the counter and behind the refrigerator, where they knew they would never be swept up. There was no longer any reason for her to stay. Blanca was not there. San Judas Tadeo could not appear to her in a broken stove. For the first time she was lost.

Esperanza ran to her room and locked the door. Without thinking, she took an ivory crucifix from the altar, the gift her mother had given her on her First Holy Communion. She had kept it with her for all those years. She pressed it against her chest so hard it made an imprint on her skin. She collapsed on the bed and tried to kiss it, but her rage engulfed her and instead she threw it down. The crucifix slid across the slippery satin bedspread, fell to the floor before she was able to grab it, and broke at an angle right below where Jesus' feet were nailed. Esperanza rushed to pick up the two pieces and kissed them.

"I'm sorry! Forgive me!" she whimpered, ashamed. "I don't know whether to love You or hate You. Why do You order San Judas Tadeo to send me on this search and then take him away when I need him the most? Why do You abandon me? Where is my Blanquita?"

After every question, she stabbed the bed with the crucifix, until she punctured the mattress. Water spurted out from the slashes, a meter high, soaking the sheets. Esperanza stared at the gushing water. She held the crucifix in her hand, like a dagger. Trying to cover the holes with her fingers was useless. The water wet the entire bedspread. It wet the floor. It seeped under the door and into the hallway, swelling the fibers of the shag carpeting and releasing the smell of rabbit piss, aged semen, discount perfume, and a faint hint of tequila.

After reconstructing the crucifix with Krazy Glue, Esperanza curled up on her deflated bed for a few hours, wrapping herself in the wet sheets and rocking rhythmically back and forth until she heard Doña Trini's shoes and her walker sloshing on the soaked carpet. She heard her knocking at her door.

"Esperanza!"

She did not answer.

Doña Trini opened the door with a key from the huge key ring that hung from her waist.

"What the hell happened here?"

"I punctured the bed."

"You should have told me immediately. If I have to replace the carpet, I'll take it off your earnings."

"I'm sorry, Doña Trini."

"And I'm sure you know what happened in the kitchen. The stove is trashed."

"Oh, Doña Trini, I'm sorry. I did that, too. I punctured the bed, I destroyed the stove. I'll pay for all the repairs, really. It's just that I get a little temperamental when I'm about to get my period."

"Well, if you're going to do this every month when your hormones go nuts, we're fucked. If Mr. Haynes weren't so fascinated by you, you'd be out of here already."

"This will never happen again. I promise."

And it never did. Because Blanca was not there. Because Esperanza couldn't afford to waste more time at the Pink Palace.

Esperanza wore her daring high-heeled shoes to Cacomixtle's motel. She had applied her makeup with millimetric precision. Her pants, previously Yuriria's, were so tight that the red color transferred to her skin, like a tattoo. It might seem she had dressed in such a way to turn him on just to turn him down. But she really wanted to show him she could become whatever she needed to be to accomplish her goal, without the aid of his hands-on teachings. And her goal was so clear in her mind that, without thinking about how to reach it, she simply set out to El Atolladero as a way of backing up to reroute her journey. Maybe Cacomixtle knew more and she just had to ask.

The old prostitute—the one with the Miss Piggy and Kermit the Frog plastic cup—walked across the bar holding a small pot of hair-removal wax to heat up in the kitchen. She wore the same hair-dye-stained robe. Esperanza's presence startled her, but she smiled politely, dragging her slippers toward the foot of the stairs.

"Liborio! She's here!" the woman yelled up the stairwell. "I told you she'd come back!" Then she disappeared behind the swinging kitchen door without a word to Esperanza.

In less than a minute, Cacomixtle was at the bar, his shirt unbuttoned, his belt unbuckled. He had quickly combed his wet hair with his fingers. Esperanza noticed a small dab of shaving cream behind his earlobe. Maybe because he ran down the stairs skipping every other step, or because he was thrilled to see her again, his chest inflated and deflated at a rate only marathon runners can maintain. Perhaps he was indeed a marathon runner. Or he lifted weights. He had no belly, unlike Scott. Esperanza noticed a little scar on his forehead where it had hit the night table during their encounter a few weeks back.

He poured himself a shot of tequila and pulled a stool closer to where Esperanza was standing.

"Want one?" he asked, smelling the thin little glass. "It's on the house."

"It's nine-thirty in the morning."

"Yeah, you're right, it's too early for tequila, but I'm out of orange juice again." He licked salt off the palm of his hand and drank the tequila in one gulp.

"So I hear you're doing well over there. The word's out. Who would have guessed; an exclusivity deal with Mr. Haynes."

"Do you have a problem with that?"

"Of course not. I'm happy to see you move up in the world. In fact, why don't you move to El Atolladero?"

"Is that what you consider moving up in the world?"

"Look, I know Trini. She's too abusive. What's she charging you, three thousand? I'll give you a break. I'll even have a special place for your little altar. Everyone's talking about it, you know that, don't you?"

He sneaked his finger under the strap of Esperanza's sleeveless blouse and lightly rubbed her shoulder to check if she was wearing a bra or not. She was. Esperanza immediately grabbed his hand, wringing it out as if it were a rag, and set it on the counter.

"Why did you send me there? It was a waste of time!" she yelled. "They don't have girls!" Esperanza's strength came out of nowhere.

"You were the one who wanted to go to Trini's. I just told you how to get there. Besides, I didn't know you liked girls."

"What are you, an idiot? Do I look like I like girls? I don't like girls! I am looking for my daughter. She was kidnapped."

Esperanza, frustrated, handed him Blanca's photo. She asked herself what was she doing there, sitting in front of such a worthless man, exposing her weakness to him and the very reason for her whole ordeal. What benefit could she get out of this absurd encounter? Obviously, he knew nothing.

"No wonder they took her. Although her mother's even prettier." He rubbed the surface of the photo, as if touching the girl.

Esperanza snatched the picture from him, disgusted.

"Do you know where she might be?"

Cacomixtle thought about this for a second.

"Looks familiar. I wouldn't doubt that they took her to the other side."

"You mean the United States?"

"Yeah."

Esperanza poured tequila in an empty glass and drank it in one big swig.

"What am I going to do? I don't know what's worse, that she's gone to the other world, or to the First World."

The alcohol burned inside her chest, like a torment. She imagined the full size of the planet with all its dangers, a slow-turning globe where all borderlines dissipated, where towns, cities, states, provinces, countries, and continents lost their sense of where one ended and the other began, multiplying the possibilities of where Blanca could be. Mexico was no longer the geographic limit to her search. Her daughter could be anywhere.

"There's a place in Los Angeles you might want to visit. The owner is my friend. He's well connected over there. He knows them all." He wrote down an address on the back of a wrinkled receipt.

"But I don't even have a passport."

"Since when has that been a problem?"

Cacomixtle looked out the window and saw Esperanza turn the corner. He was letting her go again, but he didn't feel he was losing her at all. He knew women too well from having come into this world in a brothel bed and from being raised by whores. She'd come back. Women always came back to him, whether the reason was business or pleasure. Esperanza would return, even from Los Angeles. Distance wasn't a concern, and she was better off where he was sending her than at the Pink Palace. At least she'd be out of his territory. Trini had been gaining too much power lately. She didn't deserve to have Esperanza.

Cacomixtle was attracted to Esperanza's innocence like a hungry lion to a fawn. But he knew that a predator's most dangerous prey is its own kind. His instincts sensed that innocence of hers as danger in disguise. He liked that feeling. She was crushing. Devastating. Luscious. She was addicting. And since he had recently given up chocolate to alleviate an acne infection on his cheek, he had become addiction-starved.

That she had warned him to stay away and never attempt to approach her sexually didn't mean more than a "maybe later." Women were like that. When they said "no," they meant "maybe." When they said "maybe," they meant "yes." When they said "yes," they became boring. He still had plenty to get out of Esperanza. Obviously, she had quickly learned the tricks of the trade at Trini's, and he was ready to test her. He was sure he could still teach her one or two things.

He poured another glass of tequila, but this time he savored it drop by drop, letting his taste buds go insane, warping to the touch of alcohol. A little torture was always positive for comparison before the orgy of scents and flavors his tongue and nose would soon experience with Esperanza's skin. He just had to wait. She'd be back. He licked his mustache.

Esperanza walked quickly along uneven sidewalks back to the Pink Palace, ignoring catcalling men who cruised by in their cars, demanding, "How much?" One drove a brand-new Ford. Another wore a blue suit and was listening to the traffic report on the radio, so loud everyone on the street knew the line to cross the border was estimated at two hours during peak time that day. A third had an altar of the Virgen de Guadalupe glued to the dashboard and tiny blinking Christmas lights around the windshield. The fourth one drove a Bimbo bread delivery truck. They all wanted to pick her up and take her to a motel room. She didn't even glance at them. She had too much to think about. The men soon got bored of going around the block, trying to get her to negotiate, so they each went on to their respective jobs, probably thinking, "It's too early anyway. She must be off duty."

As she walked, she reviewed her options, which boiled down to one. She would go to Los Angeles and look for Blanca there. And if she didn't find her there, she'd go somewhere else. San Judas Tadeo was not contacting her in Tijuana. Maybe in Los Angeles he'd decide to show up and give her more instructions.

She stopped at a tourist information center downtown, picked up a map of California, and sat at a small restaurant to have a cup of coffee and sweet bread. With a yellow marker, she highlighted the name of every city that got her attention: San Francisco, San Luis Obispo, San Clemente, Santa Barbara, San Diego, San Juan Capistrano, Santa Monica, San Onofre, San Bernardino.

"My saints are waiting for me in California," she said aloud.

On the way to the Pink Palace, she bought several images of her most beloved saints and a couple of statues of Juan Soldado, the unofficial patron saint and protector of illegal immigrants. He was new to Esperanza, but she liked his stiff figure, a poor young Mexican dressed in military uniform.

"He's not famous at all in southern Mexico," she explained to the man selling religious paraphernalia outside a church.

"He's a Tijuana original. A martyr. An underdog, like us. We need more saints here than anywhere else."

Esperanza needed more saints, too, now that she was about to venture across the border.

"You look like you're going to cross," said the man. "Take this Juan Soldado scapulary and fasten it on your clothes, right above your heart. My brother-in-law called on Juan Soldado as he escaped from six Border Patrol agents. Then, when he filed for amnesty, he used a scapulary just like this one and his request was approved. He owns a body shop in Santa Ana."

Esperanza took the scapulary and obediently fastened it to her blouse with a safety pin, welcoming the new saint into her life.

When she returned to the Pink Palace later that morning, Esperanza found César dragging a heavy carpet-cleaning machine out of her room.

"You should've seen the fish that came out of this carpet!" he said, breathing hard from so much exertion.

"Thanks, César, you're so nice."

"Thanks? No, darling, I'm handing you the bill."

"Please, it was an accident."

César gave her a look of disapproval that he had practiced many times before the mirror.

"Yeah, right, Esperancita. I can't even imagine what you do in this room, you bitch, with all those saints watching you."

She had never seen him so angry. Perhaps he was jealous. It couldn't be that he cherished the shag carpet.

Esperanza wondered what made him go off like that. Perhaps he, too, suffered from premenstrual syndrome.

"I've seen sexual deviations, but you're a freak!" César went on.

In her mind, Esperanza was already in Los Angeles. If Yuriria had left her wardrobe behind, Esperanza would have to leave the carpet-cleaning bill. Who knows how much money she'd need where she was headed, and cleaning that carpet was necessary anyway. She felt she'd done Doña Trini a favor.

"F-r-e-a-k!" he spelled out.

"You have no right to be rude!" she yelled.

Esperanza slammed her bedroom door, leaving César standing in the hallway. He screamed from the outside, putting his lips up against the door, like a squid's suction cups against a glass-bottomed boat in Acapulco.

"Fuckin' slut! Stove worshiper!"

"Scott?"

"Yeah?"

"No. Never mind."

"What's the matter? Are you okay?"

"Yeah. I'm okay."

"You've been kind of quiet all night."

"Can you do me a favor? Just one."

"As many as you want."

Judge Haynes parked his car on an empty Tijuana street. He and Esperanza got out. He opened the trunk. Neither of them spoke. She took off her shoes and jumped in, squeezing herself between a brand-new suitcase and her box of saints. He shut the trunk gently, got back in, and drove to the line. He turned the music up. Oldies. He liked to listen to rock bands from the sixties. They reminded him of his marijuana days when college was, most of all, an excuse to be far away from his father, who had never left Wilmington, Delaware. Scott was certain that the near-military style in which his father had educated him had determined his choice of career. But another aspect of his personality overshadowed his passion for the law. And he didn't share it with his father. Out of respect. Out of fear. He liked freedom. And he found it on the border.

He loved the contrast between Mexico and California. An exuberant San Diego filled with impeccable golf courses, right next to a barren Tijuana where dust devils never gave local housekeepers a minute of rest. Scott felt comfortable in a place where the confusion of identity created hybrid town names, like Mexicali and Calexico.

Where Chinese ate their chili dogs with green tea. Where someone had the sauciness to print "Juan López—Smuggler" on his business card. Where a dental technician brought up in Faribault, Minnesota, could find her Latin lover in an illegal immigrant who came from a tiny ranch somewhere in Jalisco. In Tijuana, Scott had screamed through the fanciest residential neighborhoods at three in the morning. He had picked several fights at El Reventón, always knocking someone unconscious. He had mingled from table to table, kissing other men's women. He had drunk himself beyond self-respect on countless occasions. And he had gotten away with it all.

The United States wasn't the ultimate free country after all. Mexico wasn't either. Instead, it was that piece of land where one met the other in an unavoidable frontal collision. But what he really loved about the border was that he could be a respectable, law-abiding, and law-enforcing San Diego judge and, in a matter of minutes, become an unidentifiable being sleeping in the arms of a prostitute, in a place where no one cared if what he did was right or wrong. And now that he was bringing Esperanza across the line with him, the parallel sides of his life were about to merge. He had found Esperanza after years of visiting Mexican whorehouses three times a week in search of a woman, other than Gladys, to share his life with. He was in love. He was willing to take the risk. And his father would never know.

His hands slid on the steering wheel. He noticed they were sweating. Things like this didn't happen to him. Not even in court. Not even when his father had caught him smoking a cigarette at age sixteen. Not even the day before, when he finally told Gladys that he had never really cared for her. Of course, he didn't tell her he was leaving her to pursue the love of a Mexican whore. In fact, he couldn't remember any time in his life when his hands had sweated. Then again, he had never helped a prostitute enter the United States illegally.

He lined up behind fifty or so cars, all waiting to cross the border. Peddlers sold miniature plaster replicas of Michelangelo's David, stone-carved birdbaths, magazines, newspapers, toys with a very short lifespan, car stereos, pirated cassettes of hit norteña bands, watches, rearview mirrors, bumper stickers, both in Spanish and English.

Everyone in Mexico knew the unwritten rule when it came to street peddlers. If you weren't interested in the merchandise, you should avoid all possible eye contact. At the slightest flicker of interest, at least three people would be shoving their wares through the window, and it didn't matter if the car was in motion or not. They were good runners, even though some had had their feet fractured by passing car tires. They must think the pain beats paying taxes, Scott thought. Since he was experienced at crossing the border, he knew the drill. He was even familiar with some of those hucksters, although their eyes had never met.

While he waited, he thought of Esperanza, snuggled among her saints in the trunk of his car. He still hadn't determined exactly what attracted him so much to that woman. She was beautiful, but he had slept with many beautiful women before. She was candid. Tender. All the mother anyone could desire. She was a mother-and-a-half. There was enough motherhood in her to keep plenty for oneself and still have some left over to give away. Best of all, he loved the taste of her skin. Spicy, pungent, tangy, like tamarind candy, especially so around her left nipple. He couldn't stop licking it. His tongue burned so much that every night after he left the Pink Palace, he had to stop at a little restaurant he knew was open twenty-four hours to drink six glasses of *horchata* with cinnamon sprinkled on it and lots of ice before heading back to San Diego.

He knew she wasn't really a prostitute. He knew she was looking for her daughter. During the nights they spent together, she had told him all about her search. The apparitions. The hospital. The doctor. The cemetery. The authorities' suspicious reactions.

How could she be looking for her dead daughter among the living? That was the one thing he did not understand. It didn't matter that her English wasn't good or that his Spanish was broken beyond repair. They had reached a state of communication that was greater than just two people understanding each other. A communion of the souls. And because he could read her soul, it was clear to him she did not love him. But if she stayed with him, he would certainly take what little she had to offer.

Inside the trunk, Esperanza prayed to Juan Soldado, holding his statue in one hand and touching the scapulary fastened to her dress, right above her heart, with the other. "Dear Juanito, I know the man driving this car is not a Mexican, but he could well be. Please help him cross the border. I haven't known you for long, but I understand you've helped thousands of immigrants reach a better life. I'm not an immigrant, but I do want a better life with my daughter back in my own town. Maybe San Judas Tadeo has already filled you in on this. I'm just going to look for her up north. If I find her, I'll come back with her. If she's not there, I'll look for her elsewhere. So, don't count me as an immigrant, but help me as one."

"American citizen?"

"Yes, sir."

"Do you have anything to declare?"

"No, sir."

Bored with his job, the young immigration officer motioned Scott to move along. Scott was uncontrollably nervous. With a jerky motion, he managed to put the car in forward gear, but suddenly the immigration officer stopped him.

"Hey! Hold it!"

Scott slammed on the brakes, causing the tires to screech. He could hear Esperanza banging around in the trunk.

"Is there a problem, sir?"

The immigration officer looked inside Scott's car. He inspected his face very closely. He looked him in the eye like he would never look at a street peddler.

"Aren't you Judge Haynes?"

"Yes. I'm Judge Haynes."

"Of course! I know you! You let my brother go off on parole last year! He was accused of smuggling pot in a plastic action figure, remember?"

Scott pretended to remember. He had to give his best performance. His career was at stake. If he was caught, he'd go to jail. Esperanza would be deported.

"That's right! I remember your brother."

"Nice to see you again! I'll tell him I saw you."

"Well, give him my regards, please."

"Sure will, when I visit him on Thursday. He's back in the joint. Only this time he smuggled some illegal aliens."

"He did?" Scott couldn't breathe.

"Yeah, can you believe it?"

"What isn't there to believe?"

The immigration officer shook his sweaty hand. Judge Haynes gave him an exaggerated grin and sped off.

Scott drove faster than he should. Esperanza had gotten out of the trunk right after San Onofre and by Las Pulgas Road was still stretching her arms and legs. She entertained herself reading the freeway signs indicating the different towns between San Diego and Los Angeles: Del Mar, Escondido, Encinitas, San Clemente, San Juan Capistrano, Santa Ana.

"Looks like it's going to be easy to get around here. Everything's in Spanish." Esperanza was amused.

"Suppose your daughter is in fact alive, why are you looking for her in a brothel?"

"Because San Judas Tadeo said she was there. I've told you already."

"When he said it, did he call it a brothel, a whorehouse, a one-night-stand motel, or what?"

"Well, now that you bring it up, I don't remember what he called it."

"Did you hear it in his own voice?"

Esperanza felt uncomfortable. Had she actually heard her saint say it, or had she reached that conclusion on her own? She was confused by the intricacies of her own explanations. She wished she had San Judas Tadeo himself sitting in the backseat, leaning forward as far as his seat belt would allow and whispering in her ear the answers to Scott's questions.

The whole conversation disturbed her. Unlike Soledad, who ruled out the apparition without a doubt, Scott wanted to believe, but he needed hard facts. Esperanza knew that in matters of faith, there are no hard facts. How could she come up with them?

"There you go again, the judge interrogating the accused," she teased, hoping he'd change the subject.

"Maybe you just imagined he said it."

"Blanca is not dead, Scott."

"If she's in the States, I can find her. There are lots of help-lines dedicated to finding missing children. You are not alone. Just stay with me and we'll look for her. We'll organize a search party. We'll have her picture on every milk carton in the nation. We'll distribute millions of flyers. We'll get the media's attention. I'll offer a reward to anyone providing information leading to her whereabouts."

"I'm so sorry, Scott. You have been very good to me, but I must look for her by myself. I already tried to involve my *comadre* Soledad, and now she doesn't believe anything I say. My priest has asked me to keep all this to myself and not involve anyone. There's a reason for it. Or has San Judas Tadeo appeared before you, too?"

"Unfortunately not."

"Well. There you have it. But you know I am thankful anyway."

Scott wondered why Esperanza was turning down such valuable help. Her chances of finding the girl, if she was alive, were better if Esperanza stayed with him. Maybe her priest was right. Only a powerful, otherworldly reason could keep her from accepting his help. A reason his mind, so accustomed to making decisions resulting from hard proof, could not comprehend. The bottom line was that this was Esperanza's private quest.

Scott checked his map a few times before they arrived at the corner of Pico and Union in downtown Los Angeles. A theater built in the twenties occupied the northeast corner. The Fiesta Theater. The marquee displayed a misspelled sign in Spanish: HOY FUNSIÓN: OJO POR OJO.

As soon as Scott parked, a young African-American man approached him with a small paper bag in his hand. Without a second thought, Scott rolled down the window, gave the man a twenty-dollar bill, and took the bag, stashing it under his seat. He hadn't smoked marijuana in at least two years. His crisis with Esperanza was enough to make him start again. He had no intentions of running for office anyway.

Esperanza thought that the young man might be San Martín de Porres, the black saint she loved so much. Perhaps he had materialized to point her in the direction of the Fiesta Theater. All the storefront signs were at least partly in Spanish. González Bakery. El León Market. Rosita Records and Tickets. The street was almost empty. She saw a wall with more graffiti than it could display, with signs that read: NO A LA 187.

"Scott, really, I have to go." The number on the side door of the Fiesta Theater corresponded to the one scribbled on the piece of paper in her hand.

"We'll rent an apartment. We can live together."

"I will not do to you what you did to Gladys. I'm sorry."

Scott realized then that he had not lost Esperanza. How could he lose someone he never really had? He began inventing reasons why she should stay with him until he had made up so many they bumped against one another in his mind, like people in a crowded elevator all trying to get out at once. He loved her. He was rich. He had resources. Confusion prevailed. Why would she want to get out of his plush new car that smelled of vanilla extract and leather and leave him, disappearing for good in such a sad-looking neighborhood? He felt the urge to hold her back. He just did not understand. He had so much to give her. How could she not love him?

Esperanza knew he did not understand. His eyes said so. The tiny tear clinging to his eyelash said so. He was a defeated bull about to lose his life in the bullring. He was a thousand men crying all at once, the last handful of dirt thrown into a grave.

Before Esperanza opened the car door, Scott scribbled a name and a phone number on the back of his business card, and gave it to her with six hundred dollars that he took from his wallet.

"The owner of this travel agency owes me a favor.

Call her. Maybe she'll give you a job." He pointed at the card.

Esperanza took the card and returned the money.

"I'll be all right."

"You don't have to be so proud, Esperanza. I don't need this money."

"Okay, just so you don't worry."

She made the sign of the cross on his forehead with the money rolled up in her hand and got out of the car. He put her suitcase and her box of saints on the sidewalk and, before leaving, gave her one last long look.

When Esperanza met Doroteo, the owner of the Fiesta Theater, he was painting a portrait of a woman in a flowing dress, exposing her breasts. She was surrounded by hundreds of eyes and thick, dark eyebrows that could have been swallows in flight. They floated in some sort of undefined limbo and turned to stare at her. The large canvas was stapled to a wall in a warehouse adjacent to the theater. The space had a deteriorated sofa that pleaded for reupholstering, a drafting table cluttered with bottles of paint and brushes, and several framed canvases leaning on the back wall. One of them was a fairly good reproduction of the Virgen de Guadalupe with a startled Juan Diego kneeling before her at the moment of the famous apparition. Blotches of paint stained the white walls, the cracked cement floor, the doors. A beam of light fell from the skylight, right between Esperanza and Doroteo, like a barrier. He moved toward his painting in a delicate kind of way, like a feather floating in the air, or like a ballet dancer gliding weightlessly across the stage, every step carefully pre-meditated and rehearsed, or so it seemed to Esperanza, although she had never seen a ballet dancer in person. A pale lavender stretch silk shirt and white slacks revealed his firm, thin torso and tight buttocks. There were no men like him in Tlacotalpan.

He took a spray can and covered a small area of the painting with dark blue. He seemed upset. Then he sprayed green. Not quite. Then ochre. He stopped.

"So, Cacomixtle sent you," he said without looking at her.

"Yes. He said he was your friend."

"That rodent has no friends. Please wait in the office, I'll be with you in a second."

Esperanza waited in the windowless office for over an hour. Old Mexican movie posters were tacked to the walls. A small picture of a nude woman dancing and a man watching her from a couch hung from a nail, doing a poor job at hiding a huge crack in the plaster. A phone rang several times. Each time a recorded message in Doroteo's voice answered: "You've reached the Fiesta Theater on the northeast corner of Pico and Union. Shows start every half hour from eight P.M. to one-thirty A.M. Tickets are on sale at the door. No one under twenty-one will be admitted. Be prepared to show your ID. If you're calling about a position as a showgirl, or if you have any other business, please leave a message after the beep." Then the beep. Then silence.

Esperanza noticed a TV set in the corner. The knobs had red and green smudges. In fact, paint stains of all possible colors covered the desk, the two chairs, and the lamp. Even the carpet had multicolored footsteps. She turned on the TV and browsed through the different channels. She found three that were in Spanish and stayed tuned to the last one.

"You won't need to speak English in California," Scott had told her. "Half the people speak Spanish here. You belong here. Stay."

He had invited her to live with him in California many times, but she was just visiting, until she found Blanca. She suspected it would take longer than she had initially estimated. Her first order of business would be to find an apartment, a decent place where San Judas Tadeo would feel comfortable showing up. She needed his guidance, his support. At that moment, she had no way of knowing if she was heading in the right direction. It was unlikely that Blanca would be working as a showgirl at the Fiesta Theater, but if Cacomixtle was right about Doroteo, perhaps he could help her get involved with the local prostitutes and obtain leads on Blanca's whereabouts.

She watched the last segment of a soap opera and wondered if Soledad was back home, watching it at the same time. A series of commercials came on. Lawyers. Family clinics. Beers. An electronics retailer. She never saw these kinds of commercials in Tlacotalpan. Then the local news. A fire had broken out on some oceanside hill she had never heard of. Firefighters were dropping water from an airplane to control the blaze. Almost two hundred homes had burned down to the ground. In another segment, a spokesperson held a microphone close up to a crying woman's face. An ambulance sped off in the background. Her boy had been killed in a drive-by shooting. He didn't belong to any gang. The mother wailed, "I should have let him sleep in!" These things never happened in Tlacotalpan. Finally came an interview with the Guatemalan president. Important people. Important events. Blanca would not be on TV. A missing girl didn't seem to be newsworthy, yet that was all Esperanza thought about. She tried to get cozy in the squeaky secretarial chair. It wasn't the ideal perch for watching TV.

Then, without a warning, like an earthquake, surrounded by vaporous clouds and sparkles and golden rays, a glowing figure, an angel, appeared before Esperanza, opening his feathered wings across the whole TV screen, as if he were trapped inside a crystal box. He was dressed in white, a belt with a huge gold medallion encircling his waist. She could see his strong body suspended in the air, descending slowly. His face was hidden behind a white mask with a glittering golden strip outlining his eyes and mouth. She heard a voice, an agitated mumble, but she did not pay attention. She couldn't help but touch the screen with the tips of her fingers and make the sign of the cross. She made the same gesture on her saints' glass cases in church back home. And she did it with San Judas Tadeo on her oven window. Now she was performing the ritual on a TV set. Then she heard the voice again. A weak murmur. It came from the TV. She identified it as the voice of a sports commentator.

". . . and El Angel Justiciero, a God-sent wrestler, challenged and beat Calambre last night!"

Esperanza didn't quite understand what the commentator was saying. She was fascinated by the angel on the TV screen, who had finally descended into a ring of light, letting go of the ropes that held him in the air and raising his arms to receive the cheers from the crowd that surrounded him. Esperanza knew this angel. She had seen him before. Desperately, she looked in her purse for the page she had ripped from Paloma's wrestling magazine and had pinned to her wall in the Pink Palace. And there he was, her angel, his image printed in the crumpled paper. She was so drawn to him that she didn't even notice Doroteo as he came into the room, cleaning his hands with a rag. Suddenly the angel's image was replaced by a soccer player who had just scored. He was running wild across the field, his bushy, curly hair bouncing with every leap. Other players grabbed him and lifted him on their shoulders. Doroteo turned the TV off.

"Sports are for those who have nothing better to do," he said. "If you're interested in the job, it's yours. I'm looking for someone with your type of features."

"What's the job about?"

"Let me give you a tour."

A huge wall, painted in an obsessive pattern of eyes

of all sizes in tropical colors, parted the theater in half and concealed the stage. Instead of seats, the space for the audience was divided into small cubicles.

"This theater is unique. There's nothing like it in the world. I built it myself. It's open every day except Mondays, like a museum. I can have up to six shows going on at the same time." Doroteo walked into one of the cubicles. "The clients can watch their own individual live show through these Sex-o-scopes. Take a look."

The Sex-o-scope was installed at eye level. It was a telescopelike tube that passed through the wall to the other side and had a lever attached to a support ring with five labeled stops: Window, Keyhole, Fragments, Kaleidoscope, and Zoom-In. Esperanza took a peek. On the other side was a tiny room with a bed and a dresser. A black woman polished her fingernails turquoise blue. As Doroteo pulled the lever to each different stop, Esperanza was able to watch the woman, first behind a semi-translucent curtain that outlined her silhouette. Then through a door's keyhole. Then multiplied by a prism. Then behind broken colored pieces of glass that moved and formed shapes as Esperanza rotated the telescope.

Finally, Doroteo set the lever on the zoom-in mode.

"With this, you can actually see the cracks on her nipple," he said.

Esperanza pulled the zoom and focused on the woman's fingernails. She needs to push back the cuticle on her right pinkie, she thought.

Esperanza set the lever on the different modes again and again. The black woman now polished her toenails.

"And what's the show?" Esperanza asked, wondering what the essence of the attraction was.

"Women wear the assigned uniform and do what they normally do when no one's watching them. They get dressed, they get undressed, they comb their hair, they masturbate, they check for cellulite spots on their asses. You know."

"And what's so interesting about this, Doroteo?"

He whispered in her ear, "The violation of intimacy."

To convince Esperanza to take the job, Doroteo had to tell her that he knew every whore and pimp in town. She asked many questions about his relationship with those people. She wanted to know if he knew any young hookers.

"I have a little friend in town and I want to look her up," she lied.

He didn't understand why she was so curious. She couldn't be a cop. She seemed too innocent for that. But he could not let her go. She was so beautiful to watch.

"I'm not only one of the best muralists in Los Angeles, but I'm one of the most respected businessmen in the prostitution industry," he assured her. "The Fiesta Theater is the place for you to start your career in the United States. I'll even provide the clothes. But first I need to see how you look through the Sex-o-scope."

Esperanza went into a tiny room. It had a bed, a night table, a dresser, and a stool. From the other side of the wall, Doroteo instructed her to look in the drawers for things to wear. The room didn't have a specific personality just yet, but Doroteo knew once Esperanza began feeling comfortable in it, she would add her own touch as the other showgirls had done. Women always altered their habitat. Carlota had created a miniature classroom. Jazmín had set up a kitchenette. Micaela had a round bed and all her walls were covered with mirrors. They provided the idea, and if it was interesting enough for Doroteo, he'd provide the construction and set decoration. Within minutes Esperanza called to him that she was ready, and as he focused in on her through the Sex-o-scope, he wondered what decoration she would come up with.

She had turned the mirror lights on. Her hair was up in rollers. The lingerie she'd chosen, glossy and dark, barely covered her thighs. She looked like a smooth, elongated copper sculpture one just had to touch when the museum guard was not watching. She tugged at her bra to cover her breast a bit more. She sat on the stool, put her feet up on the dresser, and ran her hands along her thighs as if applying body lotion.

Doroteo noticed she was trying to find the lens of the Sex-o-scope on the wall with the corner of her eye.

"Just pretend nobody's watching you," he yelled from behind the wall. "If you look at the Sex-o-scope and they realize you know they're there, you break the spell."

"I can't do this," said Esperanza to the eye behind the Sex-o-scope. "I feel like someone is spying on me."

"That's exactly the point."

The apartment building was severely cracked by so many earthquakes. Crumbled stucco exposed the naked bricks like torn flesh. The side wall had at least six layers of incomprehensible graffiti that Esperanza understood as a warning to trust no one. A double gate did not stop thieves from breaking in every other day. The building, made tired by its owners' negligence, leaned against four palm trees that grew skinny and tall in search of a blurry view of the ocean and the orange sunset that only the Los Angeles smog could produce. The place was a short bus ride away from Esperanza's new job at the Fiesta Theater.

The landlady, a chatty old Mexican woman, wrestled with the key to one of the apartments. The old lock reminded Esperanza of the one back home.

"No use trying to fix these damn doors. They come right off the frame with every quake," the woman complained.

Esperanza stuck her finger in a huge crack by the molding. Doroteo had let her stay temporarily in her little stage room at the Fiesta Theater, but the noise of the rats running around at night kept her up.

A man came out of the apartment next door. He lit up a cigarette, and the smell of the smoke blended with other odors that had settled in the hallway from the lack of ventilation. Fried tortilla. Coffee. Dampness. Insecticide. The man eyed Esperanza, who was standing by the door next to the landlady. He noticed the suitcase and the box of saints and hopped down the stairs. The landlady jiggled the key a bit harder. The door opened.

"This apartment's nicer than the other one that's available, and it doesn't face the street, so it's safer, but nobody wants it because some guy was murdered here." The landlady stepped on a dark brown stain on the carpet too large for her shoes to hide. "But it's completely furnished."

From the entrance, Esperanza could see the entire space. The woman called the place "a bachelor suite." It sounded elegant to Esperanza, but somehow the name didn't match what she saw. The sagging bed would have preferred to be a hammock. The only window overlooked an alley full of trash bins. The bathroom tile was chewing-gum pink surrounded by a grid of mildew. Several cigarette burns along the edge of the glittery Formica on the dinette table were the only vestiges of previous tenants' long and unhurried conversations. The kitchen linoleum floor had perhaps been yellow and shiny in its early years but now was dull and lifeless. The cupboard was missing a door.

Esperanza walked through the minuscule apartment, around the paper-bag-brown love seat, until she reached the kitchen. A cockroach scurried under the stove. Esperanza checked the oven window. She touched it with veneration. It was filthy. With her fingernail, she scratched off a little bit of stuck grease and smiled.

"I'd like to move in today."

*   *   *

That evening, after she closed the apartment door behind her, clutching the key in her hand, Esperanza tried hard to feel like a tenant, but she felt more like a guest. An uninvited guest. She wanted to run her hand across her bedspread, the one Soledad had knitted for her eleven years ago that now was probably being digested by moths in the linen armoire back home. She needed to smell the evening breeze that brought into her house the anxiousness of fishermen waiting to fill their nets with better days. She yearned to sink her feet in the Papaloapan River and feel the mud comfortably filling the spaces between her toes. She imagined her cat, Dominga, sniffing her slippers, still under her night table, and then falling asleep on the rocking chair to dream about getting a good back rub, the kind only Soledad knew how to give.

"It's just for a little while."

She tried to talk herself into believing she'd live in Los Angeles only until she found Blanca. Then both of them could thank San Judas Tadeo, go back to Tlacotalpan together, forget the incident, and get on with their lives. Perhaps Blanca would even marry the boy who had gone to her funeral, the one in the yellow shirt. As for herself, she could replace Doña Carmelita in taking care of Father Salvador, just as he had suggested at some point during confession. The old woman seemed ready to retire anyway, and asking Don Arlindo for her job back at the hardware store did not inspire her.

She looked around. The apartment had nothing green. She missed her patio and wondered if by now it had turned into a tropical jungle with toucans, monkeys, and iguanas, swallowed up by thick shrubs and gigantic elephant-ear leaves and twisted roots, a place accessible only with a machete in hand. She imagined Soledad walking distractedly by the ferns' leaves invading the corridor on her way to the living room, thinking about Esperanza and how she had gone crazy from grief, a disease detected only by the symptom of denial.

The rod in the apartment's closet was missing, so Esperanza left her clothes in her suitcase. She sat at the table and laid out all her saints' prayer cards. She shuffled and laid them out again, as if she were playing solitaire. She lit a candle and sat on the floor by the oven window.

"For all the love and respect I've had for you my entire life, San Judas Tadeo, for all the prayers I've whispered in your honor with my face to the pillow, show up in this filth and tell me if I'm heading in the right direction. This is not a whorehouse, if that's what's been stopping you. This is a humble, deserving apartment, and an oven is an oven, no matter who cooks what. Grease stains are grease stains all over the world. If grime doesn't care where it sticks or who cleans it, whether it's a . . . you know, a hooker fixing chicken with garlic to cure a hangover or a housewife mother of eight baking Veracruz-style cod for Christmas, then you shouldn't mind materializing in it like you did already. My strength's running out, and I have to tell you frankly that I don't feel you're being responsible. You told me Blanca was not dead. You asked me to find her. I left my house. I've searched for her in the most despicable places, and you haven't bothered to guide me. She wasn't in Tijuana. I wasted valuable time at the Pink Palace. At least you should have given me a hint. Now I'm far away from my own country. I know I should feel right at home in Los Angeles, with all these Mexicans reclaiming their land, but still, I miss my things, my town, I miss Soledad. Yes, believe me, I do. Sometimes I even wish she would have come on this trip with me. But I guess you wanted me to find Blanca by myself. Oh, dear San Judas Tadeo, how am I going find her in this city? It's so huge. Amen."

No saint, anywhere.

"Hello?"

"Father Salvador?"

"This is he."

"It's Esperanza Díaz, the mother of the dead girl who's not really—"

"Good Lord, Esperanza! Where are you?"

She was at a pay phone, next to a couple of Salvadorans who were listening to her conversation.

"I'm in Los Angeles."

"That's right by Disneyland!"

"Yes, in California."

"It sounds as if you were at the neighbor's."

"But this is very far. You can't imagine what it's taken to get here. Have you seen Soledad?"

"I've seen her about three times since you left. She misses you. When are you coming back?"

"As soon as I find Blanca. I'm working in a theater, and I've been looking for a daytime job, too, so I can make some more money to pay for our fares."

"So, you have two jobs now?"

"Not yet. It's not easy, Father. I went to a few restaurants, but they all wanted to see my papers. That's the first thing they ask for if the job is just a little decent."

"Which papers?"

"A green card. You need it to work. But as I go I'm finding out that not only is the card not green, you don't really need it to work."

"I don't understand."

"I'll explain when we're face to face. This is a long-distance call, remember?"

"Oh, dear, this must be costing you a fortune!"

"No, I paid twenty dollars in advance to these Salvadorans standing here next to me, and they say I can talk for five whole minutes."

"I'm glad to hear there are gentlemen left in the world."

"So, it seems like everyone wants the same jobs. I've been to a bakery, a garment manufacturer, a chocolate factory. Too many applicants. Too many people who nobody wants to hire. That doesn't happen in Tlacotalpan. There, you can always get a job."

The Salvadorans checked their watches at the same

time and looked around nervously as if they had done
something wrong.

"So, what's this theater job? Do you sell tickets?"

"Oh, I was going to ask you about that, Father. Am I
sinning if people see me naked?"

The Salvadorans' attention turned toward Esperanza
like a satellite dish on a rooftop searching for the signal
in the sky.

"Excuse me?" asked Father Salvador, nearly choking
on his own saliva.

"I'm not an actress. I just pretend no one's watching
me. It's like a show, but I don't have to learn any lines or
dance or anything. Nobody touches me, either. Men see
me through a machine, like a telescope, and I just do
what I do when I'm alone. I put moisturizer on my skin.
My elbows get really dry here. I stretch and do abdominals in my underwear. I clip my fingernails and push
back the cuticle. I put nail polish on my toenails. I sew
buttons back on my clothes. I pray. I read a magazine
in bed. So, sometimes I'm dressed, but other times I'm
naked."

"Esperanza, are you doing this to excite men?"

"No, please, Father. I'm trying to meet people who
deal with women of easy virtue, you know, I don't like
to say the word to you. This is the best way to get leads.
The theater owner has already given me a few names.
Influential people from the business. I just need to find
the right person who will take me to Blanca. There is
another woman working there, Carlota. Her show is
more structured. She even has a schoolteacher's desk
and a chalkboard on her little stage. She says she knows

a pimp who deals with teenagers. There's a market for them here, too, so I'm trying to get her to take me to the guy. I just want to find Blanca, Father."

"Then your objective is not to sexually arouse men but to gather information."

"That's right."

"Then I don't know how bad a sin it is. What do *you* think?"

"How bad, only God knows. It is certainly a sin, Father, I'm pretty sure of that. But it's worth it. And San Judas said, 'Find your daughter, no matter what.' I just thought I should check with you, since you're the expert. I also want to know if one can be forgiven even when remorse is delayed."

"You can carry a sin around all your life without even thinking about it. Then, on your deathbed, the sin springs up from your memory and you repent on the spot, right before your last breath, and you're immediately forgiven."

"That's a really good deal. But if death surprises you before repentance kicks in, what do you do?"

"That's a gamble you have to take as a sinner. It's all a matter of timing."

"I just hope I repent soon. I'll call you for confession when I do, or a 'confidence' if it makes you feel better. In the meantime, I'll do whatever it takes to find Blanca. The problem is that I don't even know if she is here, because San Judas Tadeo hasn't told me what to do next. He has been so unreliable. I'm very disappointed, Father. I'm running out of strength."

"Don't. Even if San Judas Tadeo doesn't appear

before you, I know he is with you. He must have a reason for his silence. Keep searching, find Blanca, and come back soon."

"I will, Father."

"I miss you, my girl."

"Are you out of your mind?"

"So what if I didn't charge her extra? You got a problem with that?"

"She talked for more than ten minutes! We could have made another twenty bucks!"

"Hey, man, I wasn't gonna interrupt the conversation. A whore talking to a priest long distance?"

"Apodaca was right. I shouldn't be doing business with you."

"Oh, yeah? Whose calling card is this? Huh?"

"It says Mandy Schwartzberg right there. You don't look like no Mandy Schwartzberg to me."

"I didn't ask whose name was on the fucking card. I asked, whose is it, and it's mine. M-i-n-e! I took her purse, not you. Remember?"

"Fuck you!"

My God, my dear God, I give up. You know why You are sending Esperanza down these strange paths. As for me, I don't understand. The doctor who supposedly kidnapped Blanca died that same week. I confirmed it at the hospital, and I told Esperanza. Not only that. Blanca's little girlfriend from school, Ramona, was very sick the week after Blanquita passed away. A virus. Why is San Judas Tadeo asking Esperanza to find the girl? Why has she decided that the best place to look is in remote brothels? I just wish You'd send her back home. But then, maybe the reason You sent her so far is to help me avoid any temptation. Are You afraid I might leave the order? So am I. After this morning's phone conversation, I am sure I want a different life. I need to be with her as many days as I have left. But I've sworn to serve You until I die. I cannot do both things. Can You help me? Can You give me strength? I have no desire to fail You. But at the same time I relish the moment when she walks into this church, luminous and without guile. I can picture her in a black dress. She knows she is alone, although every cherub painted on the ceiling blushes as she enters through the door. The light intensifies. Every candle is lit. As she tippytoes down the aisle, the breeze takes the still air by surprise and carries it out in violent dust devils. She is wearing only one shoe. It is a passion-flower-red sandal embracing her foot with straps the width of angel hair pasta. Her one heel taps on the marble floor waiting for its mate's answer, only to tap again in a senseless monologue. It reminds me of my conversations with You. She kneels in one of the front pews and, as she speaks to You more casually than I have ever witnessed before, she pulls a bottle of moisturizer out from her purse, dabs some on her elbows, and rubs it in slowly, in rhythmic, sensual strokes. She looks at herself in her compact's tiny mirror and brushes her eyebrow with her thumb. She clips her fingernails and pushes back the cuticle. She takes off her one sandal and puts red nail polish on her toenails. And I watch. I watch her through the little window in my confessional box. She doesn't know I am there. I am desperately waiting for her to lie in the aisle and do thirty abdominals, but instead, she senses someone breathing behind the cloth and stares directly toward the confessional box as if she knows I am there, watching her. She knows I have been sinning. Oh, dear God, I don't want to know what she is up to anymore. These phone calls are very dangerous. This must be the reason why the Church won't allow long-distance confessions. Amen.

The day after she called Father Salvador, Esperanza went to work early. Doroteo was painting a mural on the lobby wall. It was a madness of eyes in an explosion of colors. Spray cans, rags, brushes, and buckets of paint lay all over the floor. She showed him Blanca's photo.

"Do you know her?"

"What do you want with this girl?"

"I have orders to find her."

"It's funny, from the first day I thought you might be an undercover cop, but it can't be, right?"

"Do I look like an undercover cop?"

"Undercover cops are not supposed to look like undercover cops."

"Well, I'm not a cop. Don't worry. This girl is my daughter. I need to know if you've seen her."

Doroteo gave the photo a second look.

"I would try looking in the shelters downtown. Tons of runaway kids end up there for a couple of days."

Obviously, Doroteo couldn't give Esperanza any more leads. He hadn't even thought of the possibility of Blanca working as a prostitute.

But then he said, "Maybe she followed your foot-steps. Whores' kids do that, you know? It's in their blood."

She walked away, frustrated. Doroteo shrugged and

went back to his mural. He was no help. Blanca could not be in a shelter. In fact, Blanca could not be free or she would try to return home. But, just in case, in the days that followed, she went to six different shelters. She spoke with nuns, with volunteers, with social workers, with runaway teenagers. She went several times to one on Normandie and Pico that specialized in caring for young whores. She showed Blanca's photo to everyone. No one seemed to recognize her. She even went to the Los Angeles Municipal Jail with Carlota, the other show-girl, to talk to a pimp Carlota said dealt with underage prostitutes. But it was too late. The man had been stran-gled by an inmate just three weeks before. A dispute over a softer pillow. Carlota wept at the news, but just barely. She didn't seem to be too attached to the man, yet her tears meant her feelings for him had been stirred in some way. Esperanza was confused. She looked for a Kleenex in her purse and handed it to Carlota.

"He was scum anyway," Carlota sniffled. "And he owed me fifty bucks."

They said good-bye and Carlota got on a bus without saying another word.

Esperanza walked through tangled freeways back to her apartment. So many cars. No bicycles. People didn't go around on foot much. Where were they all going in their cars? Was anyone else looking for a daughter the way she was? Far more than the engine, a human motive in every car moved it somewhere. Women going to the grocery store, men going to get divorced. It didn't mat-ter. No one turned to look at her. On average, she saw about forty faces passing by per minute, and unlike in

Tlacotalpan, she didn't know anyone by name. She wished to see a familiar face.

Suddenly, beneath one overpass, she came across a mural of the Virgen de Guadalupe. She was glowing on a field of red roses, guarding a grave splattered with blood. A couple of guns lay on one side. A list of names on the other, all unknown to her. On the top of the painting, black words over a green banner read: "We don't forget you, Filiberto Esparza, fallen homeboy and friend." Esperanza immediately knelt right on the sidewalk.

"So you ended up all the way up here, too?" she asked the Virgen de Guadalupe out loud, hoping she'd hear her voice in spite of the freeway noises. "It's amazing what one will do for one's children, right?"

The Virgen de Guadalupe stared back at Esperanza, and a smell of roses suddenly, emanated from the wall. She took in the air, filling up her lungs in desperate need of meaning. For a long instant she felt at home. She was on her own patio, touching the delicate petals of her magnolia flowers. She thought she heard Blanca's laughter coming from inside the house. She didn't let the air go until she began to feel dizzy. As soon as she exhaled, the rose aroma was replaced with the smell of gas and carbon monoxide from the road, but she didn't care. Now she knew she could feel at home in Los Angeles, at least while she looked for Blanca.

The street looked like a street in Mexico. All the storefront signs were in Spanish. So was the music coming from huge speakers in nearly every cluttered store. Peo-

ple walking by spoke in Spanish. Newsstands sold magazines in Spanish. The smell of tacos floated on the sidewalk, luring people into tiny Mexican restaurants. But
something made Broadway genuinely American. Perhaps it was its aura of brevity. Nothing seemed to last
long there. Theaters had become churches. Churches
had become swapmeets. She imagined the place in ten
years, every sign in Korean, like the neighborhood next
to hers. Then she thought of it in the recent past, when
the language spoken there had been English, and, before
that, Spanish. For the first time Esperanza recognized the
urgency that Americans moved with, as if they were trying to catch up with the rest of the world by creating
their history in leaps and bounds. And since the United
States was free from real chaos, the substance history
was made of according to Esperanza, Americans had
efficiently made up a history filled with two hundred
years' worth of trivia. Which was fine with her. Coming
from a very chaotic country, where everyone carried
around the weight of three thousand years of convo-
luted history, she felt light and comfortable in the United
States.

Esperanza looked for an address. Viajes Paseo. It was
a very small travel agency half a block south of Broadway, on Third. A buzzer went off when she opened the
door, announcing her arrival. A woman on the phone
motioned for her to come in and sit across the desk. The
woman was large, probably twice the size of Esperanza,
and she wore a baseball cap backwards to allow a huge
bang, stiff with hair spray, to spring up from her head
like a tidal wave.

Esperanza sat and waited. The entire wall was covered with posters featuring beaches, ruins, jungles, resorts. Taped to the back wall was a life-size picture of a wrestler dressed in bright orange and royal blue tights and wearing a matching mask. His curly blond hair hung over his shoulders. He was posing in a menacing attitude. Across the bottom, his stage name: "Goldilocks."

Esperanza obediently took a brochure from an acrylic display that read: "Take One." A photograph of a table-salt-white beach bathed by artificial-looking turquoise waters reminded her of a school trip to Cozumel when she was barely a teenager. One afternoon, close to sundown, bored with building sand castles, she wandered away from the group. She picked up shells and saw how seagulls fought over a shoestring, got her skirt wet at the ocean's edge, and thought of the advantage people would have if they walked sideways like crabs. Suddenly, she noticed two boys about her age swimming naked in the transparent sea. That was the first time she had ever seen men without clothes. She remembered she couldn't help but stare, standing behind a small dune. She could tell they normally wore swimsuits by the difference in skin color between their dark backs and their pale buttocks. They played. They splashed each other. One of the boys ran against the breaking waves and discovered Esperanza standing there. He called her, his penis dangling between his lanky legs, inviting her to jump in the water with them. She stood still for a few seconds, and not really knowing how to react, she ran back to her group as fast as her feet allowed. She found it nearly impossible to run in the sand. And now, holding the brochure in her hands, it frightened her to imagine the kind of experience Blanca must have had when she first saw a naked man. She hoped with the strength of her entire soul that it was Celestino, the boy in the yellow shirt. She had always wanted her daughter to believe that sex and love were the same thing, as in her marriage with Luis. But now Esperanza knew better.

"I'll call you tomorrow. Bye." The woman hung up the phone, drawing deeply on her cigarette, and said to Esperanza, "So, are we going to send you to paradise?"

"I saw your ad."

Esperanza showed her a torn piece of newspaper with a dozen classified ads circled in red.

"Oh, great! Nice to meet you. I'm Vicenta Cortés, the owner and do-it-all of Viajes Paseo." She shook Esperanza's hand politely.

"I need a job. I know accounting."

"I'd hire you, sweetie, but unfortunately I can't decide until I've interviewed more candidates."

"Well, let me know soon, so I can tell Mr. Scott Haynes."

Vicenta heard the name and nervously adjusted her baseball cap.

"Mr. who?"

Esperanza gave her Scott's card. She had promised herself it would be her last resort. She didn't want to owe Scott any more favors, but when she saw the ad in the paper and recognized the name of the travel agency, she thought the coincidence might just be a sign from San Judas Tadeo.

"Mr. Haynes asked me to come and see you, in case there was work."

"You should have said that in the first place." She was awfully nice. "How do you know Mr. Haynes?"

"We're very close, almost relatives."

"Shit. He got me out of a fucking bad experience. I ended up in jail and he got me out. They thought I was a convenience store burglar, a fucking man. Can you believe it?"

Esperanza did believe that she'd in fact been mistaken for a man. Vicenta sat with her legs spread out, holding her cigarette tight between her thumb and her middle finger, and staring into Esperanza's eyes.

"Anyway, whatever. It's in the past. Listen, I do a little bit of everything around here: ticketing, confirmation, income tax, I exchange pesos for dollars, I transfer money to Mexico, cash checks, I sell tickets for baseball games, wrestling matches, concerts, special events, you know. It's from eleven to six. See you tomorrow."

Vicenta shook Esperanza's hand. She was hired.

February 2
Dear Soledad,
    I hope this letter finds you in good health. I'm specially thinking about you today. I know you're

celebrating the Candelaria festivities. Did they let the bulls loose on the streets this year? I remember they were thinking of calling it off, ever since that bull charged the son of Eustaquio Cantú and killed him. You must think I'm crazy for leaving Tlacotalpan. I don't write much, you probably noticed, but every day I wish you were here with me, looking for our Blanca together. I rented an apartment in downtown Los Angeles (nothing like our house, of course) and I have two jobs. During the day, I work at a travel agency. I sell tickets and send people's money to their relatives in Mexico. Then at six o'clock I go to a theater and work as a showgirl. Kind of, not quite. Don't get me wrong. I don't have to dance or do anything that requires any talent on my part. In fact, that's where I am now. All I'm doing is lying in bed writing you a letter. I'm in my underwear, but that's all right. The door is closed. All I see is the eye of some man trying to get a glimpse of me through a telescope. I think there's one particular man who comes most often. I hear him snorting behind the wall. He grunts. But he can't get close to me. He can only watch. The owner of the theater says that this is all his clients want. The owner's name is Doroteo. He is an artist. He assigned me a little room and I get to do anything I want in it. I even have set up my altar on the dresser. I've bought over twenty novena candles to light up for my saints. I put fresh carnations in a vase every other day. I've taped all the prayer cards to the mirror and placed the statuettes next to my makeup. The rosary hangs from the bedpost. The crucifix that I've glued together after

*it broke in a little accident hangs over my headboard.
Doroteo says his clients love my altar.*

*As for my plans to find Blanca, I had hoped to get
leads in this theater, but I've tried everything without
luck. I'll soon be moving on, although I don't know
where. I'm waiting for another sign from San Judas
Tadeo. He should be appearing before me any moment
now. You would be disgusted by the burnt grease stuck
to my apartment's oven window, but that's where my
saint prefers to show up. So, I spend hours sitting on
the floor by the stove, just looking at the oven without
blinking in case his appearance is brief.*

*As soon as I find Blanca, I will send you a telegram
so you can get her room ready. If you can, make her a
new bedspread with lace around the edge and matching curtains. Also, paint the room pink. Go to the
hardware store and ask for the pinkest pink. I'm earn-
ing some money. I will send you enough to reimburse
for these expenses. In the meantime, please keep in
mind that I love you. I want to say this now because it
is hard for me to say it face to face. You are my friend.
You are Blanca's godmother, and it doesn't matter if
we think differently about where she might be.*

I miss you,
Esperanza

*P.S. Drop me a line at the address on the envelope. I'll
be here for at least a little while.*

February 23
Dear Esperanza,
I'm having a very hard time writing to you. I

*started this letter three times already, but this is my
last piece of paper and the stationery store is closed at
this hour, so I hope I don't regret anything I put down
here because this is it. First of all, what on earth are
you thinking? You're letting men see you in your
underwear? What kind of sick men would want to see
your underwear through a telescope? I hope I understood wrong. If I'm not mistaken, telescopes are
machines to see stars, not bras. This whole thing is
very odd, Esperanza. Have you thought about what
your mother might be thinking of your behavior?
Remember that she's watching your every move from
Heaven. If you still believe Blanca is alive and wish to
continue looking for her, all I ask is that you come to
your senses and call the police or hire a detective. You
are not only wasting your time, you're devaluing yourself. Where is your integrity? Before, you wouldn't
even dare to hang your underwear to dry out in the
sun because you were afraid some man might see it
over the fence. Now look at you. Showing your panties
to strangers.*

*For a while I thought of going to the United States
to bring you back, but Father Salvador discouraged
me. He has told me it's impossible to cross the border
without the proper green paperwork. And then the
danger. You must have risked your life doing it. I can
imagine you running from the border guards, hiding
in sewer pipes, walking by night, and avoiding the
knife of thieves, like in the movie* Los Ilegales. *We
saw it together last year and thought it was too violent. And now you went and did it. You are not safe by*

yourself. I don't understand why you are making such dangerous decisions. I'm afraid someone might hurt you. Not everyone else is a good person like you. The world is harsh. You are safe in Tlacotalpan. Please come back. I promise I won't leave my shoes in the middle of the living room, I'll feed Dominga, I'll apply for a phone line so we can call people from our house, I'll iron our clothes twice a week. I know I'm not an easy person to live with. I complain too much. I don't help out with the chores as much as you'd like me to. But I loved Blanca like a daughter. You have been my family, my best friend ever since fate threw us together, and I thank you every day for having invited me to live with you and Blanquita. I wake up at three in the morning and go to your room. I sit on your bed. I caress Blanca's dolls. I've kept Luis' candle lit. I have one for Blanca now right next to her picture. Last week I got her one that smells like roses. The photo I picked to frame is one I took of her with you under the shade of the magnolia tree. Both of you look so beautiful. I miss Blanca and I miss you. The difference is that I can still hope you will show up at the door some day soon. I just want you to come back safe and continue with our lives. I know we can be at least half happy again.

God bless you,
Soledad

Esperanza and Vicenta were both on the phone, sitting across from each other at the only desk of Viajes Paseo. Vicenta covered the speaker with her hand to give Esperanza instructions.

"Tell her you'll check for a direct flight and get back to her."

She continued talking to someone on the other end of her line. "Yes, Mr. Peña, it's going to be eighty-nine dollars to El Paso, tax and all. But then you've got to ride the bus for four hours to Chihuahua, unless you take an Aerolíneas de la Sierra plane. Scared? What do you mean? It's a twelve seater! Yes, it's very safe. Even the Mennonites use it. Okay, you think about it and call me. Bye."

Vicenta slammed the phone down.

"Fuckin' wimp!"

Then it rang again.

"Do you think the bastard heard me?" she said to Esperanza, laughing at her own rudeness before she could answer.

"Viajes Paseo, good afternoon. Yes sir, you're in luck today. I have a few tickets left. Twenty-four bucks."

Vicenta reached for some wrestling match tickets in her drawer and rubbed them between her fingers as she spoke on the phone. Esperanza recognized the photo of El Angel Justiciero printed on the back. He was the wrestler she had seen on the TV screen in Doroteo's office.

Vicenta continued speaking, sounding anxious. "Six o'clock." She checked her watch. "Well, hurry!"

Esperanza tried to get a better view of the image on the tickets.

"Man! I almost didn't sell these!" Vicenta was relieved.

"If you have any left, I'll buy one," Esperanza said impulsively. She knew nothing about wrestling. She hadn't even been to an arena before. In fact, she had never shown any interest in the sport. But she was strangely thrilled by the idea of seeing that magnificent man in person. She just had to see him with her own eyes to believe he had real flesh and bones and hair. She didn't care what the consequences would be for not showing up to work at the Fiesta Theater that evening.

"You're a wrestling fan, too! There's nothing better. It's better than sex!" Vicenta was delighted to find someone who shared her taste. "I was gonna go by myself. But if you wanna see how they fuck up La Migra, you come with me."

Vicenta pulled two more tickets out of her drawer and fanned her face with them.

"I'll pay for both," Esperanza said.

"Get outta town! These are comp tickets. Where do you think you work?"

Esperanza followed Vicenta into the Coliseum and through the crowd. She walked right behind her, protected by her monumental mass, her indestructible gladiatorlike being. Nothing could stop Vicenta. She did not hesitate. She seemed to know exactly where her space ended and the rest of the universe began. Her sense of self was so accurate that she could tell how many centimeters long her hair was on a certain day or how wide her thighs were. Vicenta was sturdy. Esperanza was fragile. Yet Esperanza felt they could be friends.

"When I was skinny, my mom made me eat. When I got fat, she put me on a diet. So this is my way of telling her I don't give a shit about what she likes or dislikes about me," Vicenta said once, pinching the thick flab around her waist.

At the top of the stairs, Vicenta picked up two cushions and guided Esperanza straight to their seats, pushing people out of their way. She was obviously an expert in wrestling. What's more, she could have been a wrestler herself. Esperanza looked around in wonderment. All she wanted was to find out if the wrestler really did have the aura she noticed glistening around his body on Doroteo's TV set. He had seemed so large. So manly. So much.

They had ringside seats, right next to a group of men in suits bearing the symbol of some wrestling federation. People were filling up the bleachers quickly. An old woman, perhaps in her seventies, sat next to Esperanza. She wore a very tall bun that seemed to be held together with the contents of a full can of hair spray. A cascade of stiff blond tinted curls poured from the top of the bun onto her shoulders. Two seats down, Esperanza noticed three men who could have been customers at La Curva. One of them had half an ear missing. A few rows up, she saw a family with four children, all boys. They were excited, waiting for the match to begin. It should be the match of the season, according to Vicenta. La Migra had challenged El Angel Justiciero. The history of hatred between them was a well-known fact among fans. Esperanza stared at the locker room's entrance, dark and silent, a cave hiding a secret.

"The semicomplete weight brute . . . La Migra!" yelled a man in the ring whose voice crashed high up on the dome.

A masked mastodon wearing dark green shorts, an INS officer's hat, and infrared glasses jumped into the ring. His arrogant attitude was not well received by the fans. Most of them hooted. He was surrounded by a group of pretty girls dressed as policewomen in miniskirts. They danced around the wrestler and took turns kissing his biceps. The crowd screamed, "Wishful thinking!" then roared, "Loser!" and threw paper cups in the air.

"And from the heavens . . . El Angel Justiciero!" continued the announcer.

For a few seconds silence settled in the arena. No wrestler climbed into the ring. The searchlights went mad, shooting randomly all over the mesmerized audience. Esperanza was blinded. Vicenta squeezed her hand in excitement. In the darkness, a lucky searchlight finally found a winged figure hanging onto a rope slowly descending from the heights. No net beneath. Esperanza recognized El Angel Justiciero. Fog machines produced an instant cloud that swirled among rays of light and wrapped the wrestling angel as if declaring him its possession until he landed in the center of the ring.

The audience went crazy, yelling, whistling, and clapping. He was the definite favorite. He opened his enormous white cape made out of feathers to reveal his monumental body in white tights, golden shorts, a golden belt with a medallion, and sparkling green, white, and red boots resembling the Mexican flag.

"Darling!" Vicenta shrieked.

Esperanza decided that the wrestling angel was far more beautiful in person, but she didn't share this thought with Vicenta. Instead, she focused on his eyes behind the glittering mask. She would have loved to tear it off. She wanted to see the rest of this creature, untamed, powerful, ferocious, and out of proportion. She felt a pressing need to touch his flawless skin, luminescent and seductive like a flame.

El Angel Justiciero pulled off his cape in one graceful move and immediately engaged in a spectacularly choreographed fight against La Migra. Abdominal stretches, power bombs, wrist locks, leg drops, over-the-top rope dives, sunset flips, body slams, side suplexes, camel clutches, choke slams, tombstone piledrivers. Terms Esperanza had never heard before, all coming from Vicenta's screaming voice every time one of the men in the ring flew, fell, was hit or hurt.

"La Migra is a dirty son of a bitch!" cried Vicenta, without missing a moment of the high-flying war. "But the angel is a clean monster!"

Esperanza couldn't tell if they were fighting clean or

dirty. To her, they were just beating each other in a brutal dance. Most of the action happened either on the mat or on the arena floor.

"Grind his bones, Angel!" screamed the woman with the bun.

La Migra twisted El Angel Justiciero's leg in what seemed a severely painful lock as the referee yelled something at them that was incomprehensible to Esperanza. She turned to Vicenta, concerned, almost praying for the man's salvation.

"It's all right, he's not gonna die," Vicenta calmed Esperanza.

Then La Migra lifted El Angel Justiciero in the air and launched him out of the ring and into the front row. He fell at Esperanza's feet. In the second that their encounter lasted, he noticed her high-heeled shoes, her legs, and made his way up her body until he reached her face. They looked into each other's eyes, and he smiled before jumping back into the ring with renewed energy. Without wasting any time, he climbed to the top of the turnbuckle.

"He's doing a flying ax handle!" yelled Vicenta.

La Migra collapsed to the mat, nearly unconscious, but was able to yank off El Angel Justiciero's boot, throwing it at the audience. The man with half of his ear missing tried to catch it, but Vicenta was faster and caught it first. He tried to pull it from her, but she wouldn't let go.

"It's mine!" She meant it.

They each pulled the boot until the annoyed man pushed Vicenta to the steps and grabbed it.

"Looks like you've never heard of Vicenta, fuckin' asshole!" Vicenta yelled a few steps below.

As the man walked away, she jumped up and grabbed his shirt. When he turned around, she punched him in the nose. He hit her back, and they locked in a fistfight that belonged to the streets. Other spectators joined in the commotion, beating whoever was available. They all wanted the boot. Paper cups, chairs, seat cushions flew in the air. Esperanza managed to escape from the conflict, slipping between the bleachers. She had never been in a fistfight and wasn't about to start. The wrestling match continued. Those in the ring ignored the disturbance below.

Now, standing a few rows away, Esperanza saw Vicenta bleeding from her head and tried to return to her seat to help her, but the tumult had become uncontrollable and she couldn't get through. Paramedics arrived, efficiently carrying Vicenta and the defeated, unconscious spectator away in gurneys. When she heard the sirens of the ambulance leaving the arena, she realized she was on her own.

A few minutes later, El Angel Justiciero flew from the second rope and knocked La Migra to the mat. He collapsed at the angel's feet. Screaming and banging, La Migra begged for mercy.

There were thirteen two-counts, nine by El Angel Justiciero. As soon as the angel was declared victorious, and after posing for a few snapshots, he proceeded to unmask La Migra, a blond, red-faced man. The crowd cheered, and the triumphant wrestler accepted the applause, raising his arms and showing off the precious trophy, the mask. His manager climbed into the ring. He got tangled in the ropes. He gave the wrestling angel his feathered cape to put on for the media coverage. Esperanza wanted to climb up. She could have embraced the champion but waited instead for the melee to dissipate.

Esperanza walked between the empty rows of seats. The only other person left was a janitor sweeping trash. Wondering where the paramedics had taken Vicenta, she noticed the janitor throwing the angel's boot into a bin. Without being seen, she rushed to pick it up. She took out the remains of a hot dog that had been stuffed all the way to the toe space and cleaned off the catsup with a paper napkin. She would return the boot, and in doing so she'd get a closer look at the wrestling angel's eyes. After that, she could worry about Vicenta and how to get home. She didn't know the city or the bus routes. It was late. She was tired. She could call a cab. But she didn't want to leave. She held the boot under her arm and waited outside the locker rooms. She was certain that the angel hadn't left yet. She heard voices coming from the end of the hallway. She peeked in a couple of doors until she bumped into his manager, who was fixing his tie in front of a mirror.

"I'm looking for the wrestler. I have his boot."

The manager, an overweight man with greasy blond strands of hair stuck to his partially bald head, called in the direction of the locker rooms.

"Angel, are you decent?"

"It depends." His voice was soft, almost timid. It didn't match his appearance.

"Here's a lady who wants to see you."

The wrestling angel walked out of the locker rooms wearing another outfit. Obviously the gala outfit, a white spandex muscle shirt and shorts, covered by his feathered cape. A white mask enhanced by golden needlework outlined his eyes and mouth. Neither Esperanza nor the angel said anything. They looked into each other's eyes and smiled with the familiarity of two friends from childhood. The manager must have understood to leave them alone and, after giving the wrestler a big, man-to-man hug, said good-bye.

"Won't you be needing this?" Esperanza handed the angel his boot.

"You're making me feel like Cinderella," he joked. "Why didn't you catch me down there?"

"We hadn't been introduced."

"Angel Justiciero. I'm pleased to meet you."

"Esperanza Díaz."

The angel shook her hand politely, holding on to it just a fraction longer than a regular handshake.

"Can I walk you to your car?" he asked.

"I don't have a car. Actually, I don't even have a ride home. My girlfriend . . ."

"I can take you. But do you mind making a quick stop? Just for a little while. My manager and the guys are celebrating the victory at a dance club downtown."

Esperanza nodded tentatively. She was confused and excited at the same time. Since Luis, no man had invited her to dance. But, then again, the angel hadn't really invited her. He was just giving her a ride and stopping along the way. It didn't mean he was thankful to her for returning the boot. It didn't mean anything. Furthermore, why should she care if he was interested in her at all?

"But aren't you beat?" she asked.

"I can dance all night."

He held her arm. She let him. They walked together through the empty bleachers, out of the arena, and to his truck. She felt as if an entire colony of ants were marching up and down her spine. The same ticklish feeling she remembered from the first time Luis kissed her in a boat going from one island to another in the Papaloapan delta.

The dance club was filled with young Mexican immigrants dancing and drinking beer. The ceiling had Valentine's Day hearts and cupids. Saint Patrick's Day four-leaf clovers, pots of gold, and leprechauns. Mexican Independence Day flags and ornaments. Halloween witches and ghosts. Día de los Muertos papier-mâché skeletons and sugar skulls. Christmas stockings, piñatas, Santa Clauses, and reindeer cutouts. A whole year's worth of holidays reflected in the many mirrors that covered the walls.

"How do you have the strength left to dance like this after the beating you took?" asked Esperanza, very close to the angel and still wishing to tear off his mask.

"*I* took?" he asked. "How about the one I gave the nasty redneck?" He held her tighter.

The manager sat at the far-end table with a couple of young wrestlers who looked up to El Angel Justiciero. They were trainees dressed in street clothes but wore their masks. They wanted to be him. They wanted to be champions. They wanted to be dancing with Esperanza. So simple, beautiful. Beyond analysis. They sized her up. They watched her move across the dance floor. One of them, the one wearing the blue satin mask, wanted to press his flesh against hers.

Esperanza and the angel danced for two hours until, in a rhythm change, he stepped on her foot. It hurt, but she didn't care. She limped off the dance floor, followed by the angel.

"I'm so sorry!" He was concerned, aware that he could do quite a lot of damage, even when he didn't mean to.

"It's all right. It doesn't hurt much." She held her tears.

"Let me rub your foot."

He bent down under the cocktail table, following her legs. He didn't ask for permission to take off her shoe. He just did.

"Don't take it off!"

"Are you embarrassed? You carried my stinky boot all around the arena."

"It's just that I have a bad habit of losing my shoes wherever I go. And these are my favorite ones."

"It's not going to get lost here." The angel put her red shoe under his arm and rubbed her toes gently, without taking his eyes off hers. "There's a little bruise, but you'll be okay. Let me take you home."

Esperanza and the angel left the dance club unnoticed. One minute the couple was there, sitting at the table across from the young wrestlers. The next minute, another couple had taken their place and not even the manager was able to explain how El Angel Justiciero could have pulled that off.

The angel parked his '57 Ford pickup, painted with wings on each side, in front of Esperanza's apartment building. Two teenagers who shouldn't have been out so late stopped for a second to admire it. He turned down the volume on his stereo and took Esperanza's hand between his.

"I don't want to stop looking at you."

He kissed her a long time, a sensual kiss in spite of, or perhaps because of, his mask. To Esperanza, this was a different kind of kiss. Different from Luis', from Cacomixtle's or Scott's. As soon as their lips touched, Esperanza knew that this was the kiss of a man who had pursued women, many of them, out of a desire to find oneness. Immaculate. Serene. Elemental.

Both got out of the truck. The angel walked Esperanza to the door. They kissed again and said good-bye before she crossed the gate and went in the building.

The angel sped off, but half a block away he stopped his truck, drove in reverse, and parked again in the same spot.

Esperanza was not halfway up the stairs when she turned around and headed back down to the front door.

Right before she reached the last step, she heard the bell ring. It was the angel.

"I'm glad you came back, because I'm going to take that mask off," she warned.

"I dare you," he whispered.

The angel opened his feathered cape, lifted Esperanza in the air, and went up the stairs.

"Aren't you beat?" she asked. "You've danced so much."

"I could carry you up and down the stairs all night."

Esperanza had a small cassette player and a couple of tapes on the floor by her bed. The tape player was the first thing she had bought when she arrived in Los Angeles. Good medicine for loneliness was well worth the expense. She liked to listen to old boleros, preferably those composed by Agustín Lara. She felt a special closeness to him because he, too, had been born in Tlacotalpan. Hardly a week went by without her crying to the rhythm of his songs. Every time she played them, she would imagine herself and Luis riding their bikes on their way to the river before the sun came out. One particular morning, they bathed and made love on the shore grass, wet with dew, just before daybreak. They didn't miss their bed, a thick catalog of love scenes. Or the canopy, a pouring waterfall of gauze folds that kept tropical vermin and nightmares of desolation out of their sleep. A couple of bulls watched them roll on the weeds. Esperanza believed that had been the morning Blanca was conceived.

"You'll love this one: 'Aventurera,' " she said to the wrestling angel.

She turned the music up as loud as she could without distorting the sound. She waited for the tears to come out of her eyes, but to her surprise, she didn't cry.

The wrestling angel put his arm around her waist and began to slow-dance, as if they hadn't danced enough that evening. They moved centimeter by centimeter toward the bed. The candles' flames in Esperanza's altar grew to the size of lightbulbs. They flickered in excitement and painted the room with orange light. He kissed her. She kissed him back. He took off his cape and dropped it on the floor without worrying that the feathers would get damaged. She put her hands on his shoulders and slid them down his bare chest, each finger sensing his muscles like a snake caressing the terrain. He unbuttoned her blouse. She unbuckled his belt. He tried to pull down his shorts and his tights. They fit so snugly that he literally wrestled with them. He tripped and fell to the floor. He jumped back up on his feet in one graceful, agile move. Esperanza thought there might be a name for his maneuver, something like "spring-up trampoline spandex." Vicenta would know. He had to sit on the bed to undress. She sat on his lap as if it were a saddle. He lifted her skirt. And before "Aventurera" was over, Esperanza was making love in the tiny apartment she hadn't been able to call home until that moment, in a faraway city that was now so close, with a stranger she felt she had known her whole life. Even if she had never seen his face.

*   *   *

The bolero tape ended. The bed squeaked. A neighbor banged on the wall next door. A gunfight in the alley went on for a few minutes. The police came and went. The trash truck made its usual annoying beeps and clanking noises. Daylight broke. The smell of someone else's coffee sneaked in through the window. But neither Esperanza nor El Angel Justiciero noticed anything. They were still making love well into the morning, their naked bodies partially covered by the feathered cape. Finally, Esperanza untied the lace on the back of the wrestling angel's mask and slowly took it off. Before her was a man with the beauty of a Mexican movie star from the forties. But he was not in black and white, like the handsome and sensual men she had always admired in films she saw on TV when she was growing up. He was in Technicolor. In 3-D. His skin was fair. His hair was dark. His eyes sparkled and his nose had a tiny scar, probably from a wrestling injury.

"My name is Angel Galván. It's an unimaginable pleasure to meet you."

Then he warned her, "No one knows I am El Angel Justiciero, Esperanza."

He kissed her, deep and long.

"With this kiss," he said as if in a ceremony, "your lips are sealed."

They made love again.

"*Now* I'm beat," he said at noon.

Esperanza slept next to Angel. He watched her and wondered if she was dreaming about what had happened that night. The match. The dance club. Their lovemaking. He asked himself if she might have realized how fundamental their encounter had been. To him, she was like the soil of a rainforest, an enchantress, opulent and fecund. She was exuberant. She was plentiful. He couldn't disregard his excitement. He had to recognize he had fallen in love with her. To believe himself he whispered, "I've fallen in love." He then whispered it again, just to make sure. He had never heard himself say these words. He hadn't said them to Celia. They had never crossed his mind with Carmela. He couldn't have uttered them to Lidia. But in Esperanza's case, these were the only words he could think of aside from marriage, home, children. But he shouldn't go so fast. To say those he'd wait a week.

In her sleep, Esperanza set her hand loosely above her ear, as if guarding a thought that might escape. Angel hoped it was "I want this wrestler," because he needed her as much as he needed his liver, his heart, his stomach, his lungs. He had needed her, precisely her, ever since he began noticing women at age twelve. From that moment on he'd dreamt every night of the woman he'd love until death. Now that she was sleeping right next to him, he felt both relief and fear at the same time. Would she love him back? He was aware of the risk involved in loving a woman he had known for only a few hours. But his life had everything to do with risk. He didn't mind the dangers of falling for a stranger.

Angel noticed Esperanza's eyes moving fast under her eyelids. He had to hold himself back so as to not touch them. He thought of how they had kissed. How their fingers had run up and down each other's skin like pilgrims exploring a new land. And then she lay peacefully in bed by his side as if she hadn't broken anything. But she had. As they made love, he heard a crashing sound inside his chest and wondered what it was, immediately realizing she had broken his life in two. From then on, everything in his life would be placed in time as "before Esperanza" or "after Esperanza."

When Angel left, Esperanza sat alone at her dinette table near the kitchen. She waited quietly for an apparition. Even a faint one would be welcome. From her altar she took a prayer card of San Judas Tadeo and one of San Antonio, the specialist in matching couples. She rubbed both images with the tips of her fingers and prayed.

"San Antonio, please don't play a bad joke on me with this Angel guy. I just want to make it clear that I never put your statue upside down, as is customary among women who wish to find a husband. I know it works. My aunt Virginia found my uncle Sotero three weeks after she put your statue upside down. That was a pretty impressive act, considering how difficult she is. And you did it awfully fast. You must not like to be in that uncomfortable position for long. But I haven't asked you to find me a man. What if Angel is just passing by? What if I fall in love and he leaves? What if I have to leave? I don't need this, so please don't pull one over on me. I've lived all these years by myself. I've mourned Luis religiously. I can continue doing so for the rest of my life. And you, my dear San Judas Tadeo, my San Juditas, patron of desperate cases, you send me off in search of Blanca, then bail out on me, and now you send San

Antonio to put Angel Galván in my way. Is this another obstacle? Or is he going to lead me to Blanca? I can't look for Blanca and fall in love at the same time. Why don't you two get your acts together?"

With more fervor than usual, she kissed the prayer cards, made the sign of the cross, and carefully put them back on the altar.

Not even two hours had passed before Angel returned to Esperanza's apartment. He had gone home to shower and change into his street clothes and his everyday mask, the one without the glitter. He took her to a Mexican restaurant in Boyle Heights where the food tasted like his grandma's back in Chihuahua. A real find.

Angel had the habit of tracing words with his fingers. On dusty car windows, in the dirt, on bedspreads, in the sand at the beach, on his plate, but never on a woman's skin. Not until that Sunday. While they waited for their food, he took Esperanza's arm across the table and wrote "Heaven." In the following days, he scribbled all kinds of words on her body. "Explode" around her belly button. "Flame" across her upper lip. "Throbbing" on her neck. "Wild" down the side of her ribs. "Meander" along her spine. "You" between her breasts. "Portrait" on her left cheek. "Name" on the palm of her hand. "Soul" above the hairline of her pubis. "Wings" on her shoulder blades. "Sleep" on her left eyelid. "Less" on her right. "Universe" on her inner thigh. "Hope" everywhere.

That day at the restaurant, after they had the best off-season chiles en nogada Esperanza could remember, Angel expressed his wish to be with her twenty-four hours a day, seven days a week. But Esperanza refused to give up on her daughter. Esperanza spent her free time looking for Blanca in homeless shelters, brothels, night clubs, jails, or talking to pimps, social workers, bartenders, runaway kids, and prostitutes. But she wasn't ready to tell Angel about her search, or what her job at the Fiesta Theater was about. Perhaps later.

"I have a busy schedule, Angel."

As soon as she'd get off work at the Fiesta Theater, sometime between midnight and one in the morning, they would meet at her apartment, or she'd take a bus from downtown Los Angeles to Downey, where Angel owned a three-bedroom house with a large yard inhabited by a purple-heavy jacaranda and unwanted weeds that grew pretty much at will. Esperanza noticed the lack of attention to the landscaping and brought Angel some geranium plants she'd picked up at a nursery on her day off work.

"I have the feeling this house wants to be colonial blue with Indian red doors and windows," she said the first night, soaking in the bathtub, her belly floating above the foam like a peninsula surrounded by a white sea.

"Yes, I'm sure it does," he said absently, thinking about the beige color of his house. He jumped in the warm water, forgetting he was still dressed.

That was the night he discovered the tiny mole dangerously hanging on to the edge of Esperanza's belly button. From then on, that little piece of skin became his favorite square millimeter in the entire world. He thought about it every moment, even while facing a ferocious adversary during sparring, to the point where his manager noticed a drop in his performance.

"Is it the boot lady?" he asked Angel after a match.

"In particular the mole about to fall into her navel," he answered.

The manager knew to ask no more.

On the third night, when she brought and planted the geraniums in the yard, Esperanza and Angel made love in the largest room in the house. It had no furniture. Only a few dumbbells, weights, and an exercise mat. Posters of El Angel Justiciero and legendary wrestlers like El Santo and Blue Demon decorated the walls. A trophy served as a stop to the door that was being pushed shut by the draft coming in through the open windows. Lying on the mat, Esperanza and Angel first made love facing west. Then south. Then east and finally north. They couldn't get enough of their reflection in the closet's sliding mirrored doors.

"How did you get this scar?" she asked, pointing at a thin line on his skin that ran from his lower ribs toward the center of his chest.

"Somebody's knife. I was thirteen. I learned about respect the hard way."

"What about this one, above your eyebrow?"

"That was a car crash. It proved to me that no two objects can be in the same place at the same time."

"But we've been in the same place at the same time all night. How do you explain that?"

"That's different. It's the exception to the rule. We

are one now." Until one of us decides to hurt the other, he thought.

"Do you have a wrestling scar?"

"This little one, on my nose. I had an argument with my previous manager. He didn't like my style. He knew nothing about Mexican wrestling."

"Haven't you ever been hurt by another wrestler?"

"Not really. I just had my pinkie broken once, but the damage is inside. There's no scar."

"Sometimes that's the kind of damage that hurts the most."

"You bet."

The word *loss* came to Angel's mind, but he didn't dare to write it anywhere.

"Let me get this straight. You're skipping training this afternoon because of the boot lady?"

"What can I say?"

"I hope you realize what this distraction might be doing to your career."

"You've seen me with other women. Many women. Since you and I started working together I've been involved with at least seven."

"Seven! I never thought you'd count Celia."

"Just because she's your cousin?"

"You only went out with her a couple of months."

"Still counts. They all count. But Esperanza is different."

"But you're losing focus. You've said many times that wrestling is all you care about. Do I have to remind you? Think of the pain you felt when you left Chihuahua to train in Mexico City. Remember what happened with your family. What did they do when you told them you wanted to be a wrestler? Have you forgotten? Your mother stopped talking to you. Your aunts. Your grandmother. Your sister. Your dog. And now you're wasting it all because of a woman."

"She's not just a woman. She's my woman! And I'm only skipping two hours, for Christ's sake! We're buying a sofa. I want her to pick it out."

"I'm just worried that this might get out of control. I don't want your ass to get beaten. You're almost at the top. Imagine what your father must be thinking about all this, watching you from above. Imagine the headlines if you fail: 'The son of the great Máximo Max—who died courageously in the ring before the eyes of his wife and children—abandons his spotless wrestling career to pursue the love of a woman.' "

"Have I ever let you down at the arena?"

"No."

"Have I ever stepped on the memory of my father?"

"No."

"There you have it. Now let me go get my new sofa."

An eye looked at Esperanza through the Sex-o-scope. The same eye that had been spying on her for the past two weeks. She wore a scant nightgown and read a wrestling magazine in bed, occasionally grabbing a tortilla chip from a bag. The altar had grown in size. More saints in frames. More crucifixes. Forty-two novena candles. Sixty-eight prayer cards. Nineteen statuettes of different holy figures. Three flower vases with carnations. A framed image of the Virgen de Guadalupe. Her glow-in-the-dark San Miguel Arcangel. There was barely any room left for her.

The eye blinked. With a sidelong glance Esperanza searched for the hole in the wall. She got up calmly, sat at her dresser, applied a cleansing cream to her face and wiped it off with a tissue, walked across the room toward the blinking eye, took her shoe off, and stuck the spiky heel in the hole to obstruct the view from the other side. She was through with that job. She would quit that day and look for Blanca elsewhere. This was another dead end.

"Fuckin' whore!" she heard an angry man scream behind the wall.

She went back to bed, ignoring the man until he burst into her room, nearly tearing the door off its hinges. She recognized the infuriated visitor as he was shaking her and pushing her across the room. It was Cacomixtle.

"You bitch! Why do you think I come all the way to L.A. and pay my money every week? To see a goddamn heel?"

He slapped her across the face. She fell on her altar. Novena candle holders shattered on the floor. Saints broke. The mirror on the dresser was smashed. Her prayer cards scattered.

"You knew it was me behind the wall! Didn't you?" He hit her again.

On the floor, Esperanza used her arms as shields to protect her head from the blows. She tried to get up but had no strength.

"That's how I wanted to see you, slut!" He unbuckled his belt. He unzipped his pants.

From an unknown place and force, perhaps Luis' soul watching over her from Heaven, strength came to her in the form of a wave of rage, running up her body and ending in her fists. She picked up a broken statue of San Martín de Porres, whispered, "I'm sorry, I'll fix you later," and slammed Cacomixtle in the testicles. As he writhed in pain, she threw the night table at his head, leaving him almost unconscious. Now he would have another scar on his forehead, this one right above the left eye, across from the previous injury. When it heals, Esperanza thought, it will look as if he'd had a pair of horns amputated.

"Filthy whore!" He was breathless.

"That's how I wanted to see *you*, Peeping Tom!" she yelled.

She quickly dressed, blew out as many candles as she could, picked up the remains of her altar, and threw her saints on the bed, joining the four corners of the bed-spread to form a sack. On her way out of the room, she kicked Cacomixtle in the head.

"And this one's for making me waste my time at the Fiesta Theater! There are no girls here either!"

San Pascual Bailón and San Martín Caballero fell out of the bedspread, and she came back to pick them up. On the way to the door, she found Doroteo, painting a wall in the lobby.

"Jesus Christ! What happened to you?"

Shocked, he stepped back and nearly spilled a can of paint he had sitting on a stool. His mural had already invaded the hallway.

"I had a little argument with your friend from Tijuana."

Esperanza looked for the room's key in her purse, trying to hold the bedspread with her prayer cards and broken saints at the same time. A candle depicting the Powerful Hand, famous for protecting the innocent, fell through an opening and shattered on the floor. Finally she found the key and put it in his palm.

"I quit."

"Goddammit!"

He launched the key into the air. It smashed through the concession stand glass case and ended up among shards and packs of M&M's and Hot Tamales.

"Just when you were becoming famous!"

Esperanza didn't answer. She ran out of the theater and headed for the corner. The roughness of the sidewalk on her feet made her realize she had left her shoes behind. They weren't her favorite ones anyway. She looked back and saw Cacomixtle and Doroteo catching up with her. Just when they were a few meters away, Esperanza jumped on a bus.

"Fuckin' bitch!" Cacomixtle screamed, breathless, from the sidewalk.

Doroteo threw a bucket at the bus as the door shut, splattering red paint all over an advertisement of a horror movie involving giant mutant cockroaches.

"Women!"

"What did you do to her to piss her off like that?"

"We had a little issue from Tijuana. No woman's ever gotten away from me before, but she's done it twice."

"I'm tellin' ya, no one should ever talk to women. Only watch them through the Sex-o-scope."

"The bitch. This is it. I'm through with her."

"I'd say she's through with you. Now what am I gonna tell my clients? They all wanna see her stupid altar."

"Paint one."

The image Esperanza saw in the mirror scared her. Her right eye was nearly swollen shut because of a large bruise high on her cheek, and she had a small cut along her left eyebrow. She had reacted in self-defense, and that was something to consider in her moment of repentance.

It was time to rethink her strategy. She had failed at the Pink Palace and at the Fiesta Theater. Her saint was more silent than ever. She looked awful. She couldn't show up at the travel agency in such a state. She felt like crying on Angel's shoulder while he rubbed her back and stroked her hair.

A knock on her door startled her. Maybe Cacomixtle had followed her home. Quietly, she tiptoed to the kitchen and found a ridiculously small knife. A paring knife. Her only knife. No peephole. She put her ear against the door. No noises. Another knock. No answer.

"Esperanza!" It was Angel.

She covered her black eye with her hair and opened the door, relieved, but Angel noticed the cut and bruise right away.

"What happened to you?" He quickly took off his satin mask and stuffed it in his shirt pocket.

She didn't answer. She just hugged him and wept on his shoulder. Her tears rolled down his shirt and into his pocket, getting the mask wet. He rubbed her back and stroked her hair.

"Don't tell me if you don't want to."

After crying and sobbing for a while, Esperanza agreed to put a raw boneless chicken breast on her injury. A steak would have been better, according to Angel, but one had to work with what was available. Red meat was expensive.

"This will take care of it. You'll see. I'm an expert in bruises."

Angel studied Esperanza in detail, as if he wanted to cure her with his eyes. She felt uncomfortable.

"You need more than cold chicken. I'll be right back," Angel said. "Don't go anywhere."

As soon as he walked out of the apartment, Esperanza had a frightening feeling. The same feeling she had when she lost her father to the flood and her husband to the bus accident, both having left her in circumstances they could not control. She feared for Angel's well-being. Would he leave her, too, even if he didn't mean to?

When he came back, she was right where he had left her, still holding the chicken breast to her face and wondering how she ended up falling in love in the middle of her search for her daughter.

Angel opened a tube containing a bright blue ointment that he brought from his truck.

"I always carry this in my glove compartment. Life hits hard sometimes and you have to be ready."

He applied it under the chicken breast and around the rest of her bruised face.

"How long have you lived here?" Esperanza asked, trying to distract herself from the pain.

"Fourteen years."

"No wonder you're more gringo than a cheeseburger and fries."

"Yeah, but with a lot of jalapeños. I can't just stop being Mexican, so I've become amphibious. I go back and forth from Mexican to American, depending on the situation."

Angel put the tube in his back pocket.

"The closest place you can get this ointment is at a veterinarian pharmacy by the racetrack in Tijuana. It's the best for muscle pains and bruises. Just ask any horse."

Esperanza tried to smile, but it hurt.

"Are you ready to tell me what happened?" he asked, carefully holding the chicken breast in place.

Esperanza's voice cracked with exhaustion and sadness as she finally told him about Blanca and her search. About San Judas Tadeo. La Curva. El Atolladero Motel Garage. The Pink Palace. The Fiesta Theater. And her fight with Cacomixtle.

Angel dried her tears using his mask as a handkerchief.

"You don't have to believe me if you don't want to," Esperanza sobbed.

"I believe you."

Esperanza stopped crying.

"Everything?"

"Everything."

"Even the part about San Judas Tadeo?"

"Even the part about San Judas Tadeo."

"That's odd."

"I don't see what's odd about it. On the contrary. What else would drive you to do what you've done? It has to be on orders from above."

"But I'm getting so frustrated."

"You'll find your girl sooner or later."

"But I've lost contact with my saint. I don't know what to do next."

"How has he appeared before you?"

"His face forms on the grime of the oven window."

"Here or back in your hometown?"

"There."

"Have you told anyone?"

"The priest in my parish, my *comadre* Soledad, and an American friend from San Diego."

"And me."

"So that's my secret. I didn't scare you off?"

"Hell no! Nothing scares me anymore. Not even Vaca Sagrada. He is trying to unmask me in the ring, but he's not going to get away with it. I have Mexican training and he doesn't."

"Well, then we must light a candle."

"Two candles. One so I don't get beat up and one so you find your girl."

"I've lit plenty of those already, but one more wouldn't be too much. Maybe San Judas Tadeo needs more candles to show up. I want him to see my altar." She blew her nose.

"He'd be impressed, I'm sure."

"I have his image in all kinds of forms. Inside an acrylic pyramid, on a key chain, in a plastic capsule to keep in my purse, on prayer cards of many sizes with different prayers printed on the back, for the road and for desperate cases," she recited, counting on her fingers, trying not to forget to mention anything.

"I also have statuettes made out of plastic, clay, plaster, all sorts of materials. He is always wearing his green robe and has a flame flickering out of the top of his head. One of my San Judas Tadeo statues has a tiny lightbulb built into the head and it flickers. I have to change the battery every now and then, though. He has real eyelashes. Look at it over there." She pointed at the table where she had set up her altar.

"Is this something new to you?"

"I've loved my *santitos* ever since I was a little girl. But I've collected most of this stuff since he appeared."

"Do you buy it at the stands outside churches?"

"I got most of it in Tijuana. That's a big market for San Judas Tadeo. There are many desperate people there. But now I need to find some new ones here. I lost quite a few during the argument I had with the theater client."

The theater client. For a second she thought of Cacomixtle. Scott. César. Doroteo. The tall guy from La Curva. All the men she had met while looking for Blanca. Sometimes she didn't recognize herself anymore. Maybe Angel would help her understand all those experiences. Right then, the events were too recent to analyze. To separate into fragments, study, and put back together so she could accept them as part of her life. At this point, they were too close and all she saw was a blur, as happened when she tried to look at a picture of Blanca one centimeter away from her face. If she wanted to see the details, she had to hold the picture at arm's length.

"I know a church downtown that has a beautiful life-size San Judas Tadeo. Some people say he has talked back to them. You may want to visit him tomorrow," said Angel.

Esperanza nodded and cuddled up on the couch next to Angel. He embraced her. They fell asleep. They woke up at two-thirty in the morning, freezing cold. He had a backache. She had a stiff neck and her face throbbed. She threw the chicken breast in the trash. They dragged themselves into the bed. They made love. He proposed.

"Esperanza, you're my Eveready, my Energizer, my Duracell, my Aguila Negra. Marry me. I want us to have a baby boy. Or a baby girl. Or, better yet, twins."

She answered by suggesting names for their future

children: "Daniela. Natalia. Ximena. Fernanda. Andrea. Diego. Rodrigo. Santiago. Nicolás. Sebastián."

They fell asleep again.

Esperanza walked into the travel agency quietly. A small gauze bandage covered her check, but her eye was still swollen. Vicenta was on the phone. Esperanza didn't want to distract her, but the buzzer at the door gave her away. Vicenta put out her cigarette in an ashtray full of butts.

"All right, I'll book a seat for your mother, but are you sure you want her in another row?" With her hand she brushed ash that had fallen on the desk as she spoke to the person on the line. "Yeah, I know, it's a pain in the ass. I know someone who throws up, too. Okay, whatever you say. Bye."

"I'm sorry I haven't been to work these past few days."

"What the hell happened to you?" asked Vicenta, touching Esperanza's injury with the tip of her thumb.

"Some jerk."

"I was wondering about you. Go home, dear. You don't want to work like that." Then she said to herself, "Unless you're a fucking business owner, like me. Then you really exploit yourself."

"I brought you something that I thought you'd like to have." Esperanza took El Angel Justiciero's green, white, and red boot out of a shopping bag and put it on the desk in front of Vicenta, like a trophy.

"How the fuck did you get ahold of this beauty?"

"I've been seeing the angel, pretty much on a regular basis, and last night I told him about you and how you got beat up over his boot, and he said you could have it. He wrote his autograph on the sole."

Vicenta read aloud, "To Vicenta in gratitude. El Angel Justiciero," and hugged the boot. "You're going to Heaven, sweetie!"

Esperanza went alone to the church downtown that had a beautiful, life-size San Judas Tadeo. Unlike Scott, Angel instinctively knew to stay away from her search, but he did give her directions to the church he knew had a San Judas Tadeo.

The main image in this church was the Virgen de Guadalupe. She was formed by a composite of snapshots of the original painting hanging from the altar at the shrine in Mexico City. The snapshots were glued side by side. It looked fragmented but whole at the same time. Certain parts were a bit off, maybe on purpose. A modern interpretation, different from what she had seen, but she liked it. At the base lay nine wedding bouquets in different stages of decay, left by the brides who had come to offer them to their Virgen de Guadalupe the previous weekend. She remembered when she and Luis had gone to the shrine in Mexico City so that she could offer her own bouquet. Hers had been a single light purple hydrangea twice the size of a head of lettuce cut fresh from the original shrub her grandfather had planted on her patio. At the last minute, before going to church, Soledad had tied a white bow around the stem.

Standing among the hundreds of parishioners visiting the Virgen de Guadalupe at the shrine in Mexico City the day Esperanza went to offer her wedding bouquet, she had prayed for a long and loving marriage. And because she had been an only child and had lost her parents at an early age, she had prayed for a large family as well. At least three children. That was the minimum. Just enough to fill her house with laughter. And a few quarrels and tantrums, as was natural. But now, in front of this new image of her beloved Virgin, she thought that perhaps her prayers had taken a wrong turn and had gotten lost among the clouds on the way to Heaven.

Now she was in a faraway church, pleading for the return of her only daughter. Her only family. What if her whole life went by looking for Blanca? The thought scared her. She hoped to have her girl back at least for one day before dying. A few hours would do. She found her saint standing on a pedestal in an arched niche too small for him. This San Judas Tadeo was indeed brand new, unlike the one in Tlacotalpan. The golden embroidery along the green tunic glittered. Little tin hands, legs, cars, and houses were pinned to the cloth, along with many photos of children and old people. His eyes were shining. They looked real, not like marbles. His hair was synthetic, like a doll's. His sandals were a bit big for his feet. She lit a candle and knelt with deep devotion. Perhaps he would talk now.

"You know I've been trying to make contact with you in every oven that I've come across. I've searched for the grimiest ones. In brothels. In restaurants. In rented apartments. No luck. I left my house, my town. I've had to put up with men's sexual desires to get information you could have given me so easily, in a plain old apparition. I've tried to decipher your riddle. Yes, Blanca is not dead. I understand that. But where is she? Are you only going to appear before me in my oven at home?"

At the precise moment these words left her mouth and spilled out into the air, a blinding light filtered in through a purple stained glass and fell on her face. She looked up toward the window and squinted. The day was overcast, the other windows were dark, yet that purple light was as bright as the sun in mid-August. She heard the faint sounds of a choir practicing a song somewhere up on the roof. "Hallelujah! Hallelujah!" She imagined the members of the choir clinging to the gargoyles, dangling from the gutters, and singing at the same time. Baritones. Sopranos. Tenors. All together in a hymn of joy only for Esperanza's ears to hear. San Judas Tadeo's tunic fluttered with a draft that came in through the sacristy door, the flame at the top of his head glowed, and she saw how his foot had grown to fit the sandal. Esperanza realized that what she had just said had actually been a message from her saint.

"In my oven at home," she repeated.

Esperanza rose quickly, kissed San Judas Tadeo's toe,

made the sign of the cross, and ran out of the church, leaving an echo of footsteps bouncing off the walls.

Esperanza didn't say good-bye to Angel. She didn't even have time to quit her job at the travel agency. She took a bus to San Ysidro and crossed the border back into Mexico on foot, tightly holding the patron saint of illegal aliens, Juan Soldado, against her chest. She was surprised to find how easy it was to cross back, as opposed to going into the United States. No one bothered her. The immigration officers seemed to be happy to see all those Mexicans willfully going back home. She walked among the crowd along the bridge that links the two countries, followed by two young men who volunteered to help her carry her box of saints, which had nearly doubled in size. She also carried Cacomixtle's tote bag with one change of clothes, including her favorite shoes, the ones Scott had given her at the Pink Palace, wrapped in tissue paper. The rest she left in a trash bag on the apartment floor with a note that read: "For the shelter on Normandie and Pico."

On the Mexican bus back to Tlacotalpan, she imagined Vicenta wondering why such a responsible employee would disappear without a reasonable explanation. "She didn't even pick up this week's paycheck!" she could almost hear Vicenta saying to herself.

She also imagined Angel going to visit her, as he had done every day for more than three weeks, not knowing she was gone. He would find the envelope with the rent money and the apartment keys. He would look for a note addressed to him. He would turn the whole place upside down looking for a damn note that read: "Dearest Angel, I'll be right back." But there wasn't one. Not because Esperanza didn't want to explain to Angel why she had left in such a rush, but because of the rush itself. She would write as soon as she got home. As much love as she had to give him, she couldn't promise him anything then. She was awaiting orders from her saint. So she sat quietly on the bus and prayed.

"Dear San Judas Tadeo, why didn't you tell me before that you would only visit me on my oven at home? I've spent months looking for Blanca in all the wrong places." She pulled tissues from a family-size box of Kleenex to wipe the tears she had shed in the last few hours. "Was this trip part of the plan? Was I supposed to go away just to come back for the real directions? I hope you give me accurate clues this time. Telling me she's not dead isn't enough. I must know who took her, where to look for her, and how to get her back." She let tissues fly out her open window every other minute. From the outside, they looked like pigeons rolling out of control in the bus's exhaust. "The world is huge. Have you forgotten? You must remember when you were once here in flesh and bone. You traveled on foot and preached throughout Mesopotamia, converting Persians to Catholicism. I'm sure you thought then that this place was vast. Imagine trying to find one little girl. Imagine trying to find her in brothels."

Next to Esperanza sat a man from Chiapas. He was a hunting guide. He told her he knew the jungle like the palm of his hand. His right hand, that is. He had lost the left one a few years back. He had chopped it off himself with a machete when an anahuyaca had crept up from the mud and bit him between his thumb and forefinger. It was the only way he could survive the deadly venom.

"I was also bitten by a snake. The snake of evil," Esperanza said.

She felt no remorse now, but it would have to sink in someday, just enough to be forgiven for lying to all those men and making them believe she was what she was not. She had clearly heard her saint say "Find her, whatever it takes." Then again, what if San Judas Tadeo had purposely placed her in all those compromising situations? What if his intention had been to temporarily separate her from Blanca, make her leave her hometown and end up in sordid places just so she could put in perspective the amount of pain involved in ironing a pile of clothes? Sometimes saints made people go through Hell so they could appreciate Heaven.

The handless man in the bus cried for his missing hand. Esperanza cried for her missing daughter. They shared the box of Kleenex. They were friends for a few hours. He got off in Veracruz. She continued to Tlacotalpan.

*　　*　　*

The town floated at the edge of the river. A tropical storm had hit two days before, another passenger told her. The road was closed. Vehicles stood abandoned by the side of the cracked pavement. The sugarcane fields were snarled, ravaged. But to Esperanza, the devastation she saw outside her window was delightful. She was home.

She got off the bus when the sun was going down and waited by the bridge for a boat to take her into town. In the distance, she could see some lights shimmering on the water inundating the streets. This meant that the flood hadn't been as disastrous as others in the past. Electricity had come back in less than forty-eight hours. This was either a huge accomplishment by the power company, which was doubtful, or the downpour hadn't really been so catastrophic. By Esperanza's estimate, Tlacotalpan could get its streets back in a couple of days, when the river returned to its normal size.

"I can only take one person!" cried a man on a feeble dinghy approaching the shore.

Esperanza looked around. There was no one else but her. That made the decision easy. She got on the tiny boat and thanked the man.

She held on to her box of saints so it wouldn't fall overboard. The town's lights drew closer. She knew one of those lights came from her house. The TV set, for sure. She wondered if Soledad was watching a soap opera or had fallen asleep.

Esperanza disembarked on the dock, carrying her heavy box on her head. The water lapped only up to her ankles. She walked slowly, leaving a tiny wake behind her feet. The streets seemed narrower than before. The colors of the houses appeared to be much brighter, even at dusk. Very different from the wide streets of Los Angeles and the dull colors the Americans liked to use to paint their homes.

The strap of her left shoe came off. The drenched sole on her right shoe detached from the leather. One more pair she'd have to replace. The box got heavier, probably because her saints were loading up with meaning as they got closer to her home. Esperanza walked past the hardware store where she used to work. It was closed. She walked past the house where Celestino, the boy in the yellow shirt, lived. The lights were out. The cemetery was on the other side of town. The church was not on the way. She'd go first thing in the morning.

After a few streets and alleys and turns to the right and to the left, she nearly walked past her home. It wasn't egg yolk yellow with bougainvillea pink lines around the doors and windows anymore. It was water lily purple with orange bird of paradise patterns around the doors and windows. She had a strong feeling of discomfort. She hadn't chosen those colors. She hadn't leafed through the paint catalog. She hadn't made any pigment combinations. She hadn't poured samples of the paint into baby-food jars and brushed it in small patches on an exterior wall, checking how the sunlight affected the color throughout the day. She hadn't made sure the colors were unique in the neighborhood. She looked at the house again. It was the same house, but it felt like someone else's.

The curtains were pulled shut. She couldn't see

inside. She felt guilty for trying to take a peek. She stepped up to the dry portico. Her box of saints was safe. She knocked. She didn't have a key. A long minute went by. The door opened.

"My God! Oh, my God!" Soledad looked five years older, more gray hair, more wrinkles around her eyes. And she still sounded concerned.

"Look at you! Just look at you!"

They hugged. They laughed and cried at the same time, just as they had done before Esperanza's wedding when they were fixing her bouquet.

They went inside. Her grandfather's hydrangea and the orchids in the patio's terra-cotta pots were overgrown. The magnolia tree needed pruning. The hibiscus had spiderwebs. Esperanza knew her plants had suffered neglect, but she was so happy to see Soledad that she didn't mention it. They sat in the living room, each with a fly swatter, and as they whacked mosquitoes like professionals, they filled the dark gap between them created by the lengthy months of separation.

"What in the world were you doing in all those brothels?" Soledad was outraged.

"Looking for Blanca. I've told you before."

"And for that you had to work as a prostitute?"

"It was the only way I could get to her."

"Why didn't you ask around, like any decent person?"

"I did that, too."

Esperanza knew Soledad would not condone her behavior. She wouldn't even try to convince her. Beetles crashed against the screens, tempted by the living room lamp's light. Mosquitoes buzzed by the women's ears in death-defying stunts. They didn't hear the crickets' noises, more obtrusive than ever. A neighbor's loud radio announced the tropical storm's update. As usual, it was heading north to hit Florida. Esperanza was thrilled to hear these sounds again. It was this absence of silence, this eternal whir, that made her feel so at home.

"Esperanza, what's it like?" Soledad spoke almost whispering, embarrassed, perhaps hoping not even Esperanza would understand what she was asking. "I mean, how does it feel? What's it like to do it with a man who's not Luis?"

Esperanza stopped swatting mosquitoes and looked into Soledad's eyes.

"When an angel falls from the sky and lands at your feet, you realize that you have a chance to love once more."

"An angel? Another one of your apparitions?"

"He's a man. He's an angel. And his name is Angel. I can describe to you every centimeter of this man."

"I can't even remember the color of Alfredo's eyes," Soledad said, still nostalgic, but resigned.

Esperanza held her hand tightly, anticipating a couple of tears that did not materialize.

"Do you remember Don Remigio Montaño, Blanca's guitar teacher?" Soledad's voice changed, suddenly revealing a hint of cheerfulness, absolutely foreign to her usual tone of preoccupation. "He brings me a red carnation every day. He composed a song for me, and he sings it every night at the restaurant where he works. It's called 'Welcome to My Heart, Soledad.' He asked me to marry him."

"Will you?"

"I've been waiting to tell you this for so long. He proposed after you left. I didn't want to leave you. You were not taking Blanquita's passing well at all. I thought you needed me, but when I saw that you were not coming back, I said yes. Can you believe I said yes to a retired mariachi?"

"This is the best news I've heard from you in years."

"Aren't you concerned?"

"Why should I be?"

"Maybe I'm the one who's concerned. Now that you're back, I don't know if I should stay with you or marry Remigio."

"You can't keep on watching over me, Soledad. I am fine. I am not sick. I am behaving just like any other person would in the same situation."

"But I'm worried about you."

Esperanza was tired from the trip, surprised by Soledad's news, and eager to visit her kitchen oven. So she invented an excuse.

"We need to talk about this. I'll get us some water. Wait here."

She went straight to the oven and found that it had been cleaned spotless. Not a speck of grease. Not a drop of grime.

Esperanza knocked over everything in sight in the pantry until she found the can of Easy-Off. She grabbed it and ran back to the living room, where Soledad was beginning to open the box of saints.

"What did you do to the oven?" Esperanza was furious.

"What do you mean?"

"Don't play dumb! With this!" Esperanza showed her the can of Easy-Off, holding it like a gun.

"I cleaned it, what else was I going to do with it? It was so greasy it almost caught on fire."

Esperanza couldn't contain her rage and threw the can of oven cleaner out the window, smashing the glass.

"Now I'm fucked!"

"Esperanza! Open the door!"

"No!"

"You can't just stay in the bathroom forever!"

"Yes I can."

"Please, let me in."

"No."

"I'm sorry. I shouldn't have cleaned the oven, but it was filthy."

"You did it on purpose. You don't want me to talk to San Judas Tadeo. You don't want me to find Blanca. You don't believe me. You never have. You think I'm making all of this up. Just leave me alone."

"Esperanza, I believe that you believe. And I hope that's enough for you because that's as far as my faith goes. I understand you now. I've thought about it a lot. Please forgive me. I don't have the power that you have. Not all of God's children have your capacity for faith. I'm handicapped in that respect. You are lucky. Faith is the most powerful shield against the worst, and you have it. But you cannot force someone to believe. Please don't ask so much from me. And I promise I won't make it all more difficult on you."

"You mean it?"

"I mean it."

"You'll stop judging me?"

"I swear. Now open the door."

The sun was out and puddles evaporated everywhere, producing miniature clouds that lingered above the rooftops, hanging on to the tiles, as if they were afraid of going through the traumatic experience of becoming a storm again. Almost a week had gone by since Esperanza's arrival home. She walked hurriedly down the sidewalk. She wore brand-new shoes. Sunflower yellow high-heeled shoes. Don Arlindo, her ex-boss, walked toward Esperanza in the opposite direction and passed her without recognizing who she was, but he did turn around to check out her behind. Esperanza knew he'd do exactly that and turned her head quickly. Caught red-handed, he accelerated his step, embarrassed, and disappeared around a corner. Esperanza smiled. That man seemed so small now. How could she ever have feared him?

She went inside the church. All her saints were still there. San Pascual Bailón had been attacked by termites and two fingers were missing. San Martín de Porres' black robe was faded. The Virgen de la Candelaria had lost a marble eye, and all that was left was the empty socket. None of them came to life for Esperanza.

Fidencio, the sacristan, was up on the choir cleaning the organ. He looked down the balcony and recognized Esperanza walking along the side aisle. He was about to call her name, when he remembered that he was mute. He didn't have enough time to run and warn Father Salvador. She was heading straight to the sacristy. Fidencio rushed downstairs. He followed her and stood outside the door. He couldn't miss this confession.

Esperanza found Father Salvador fixing Santo Niño de Atocha's chair. Several other saints awaited repair in the crowded room. A soap opera rerun filled the TV set. He wasn't watching it.

"God Almighty!"

Unlike Don Arlindo, who could not see beyond physical appearance, Father Salvador recognized Esperanza on the spot.

"I've missed you so much!"

He hugged her respectfully. A very long hug. He needed to make up for all those he hadn't been able to give her over the phone.

"Where have you been, my child?"

"In Los Angeles since we spoke last. But I'm back. Very happy to be back."

"Thank God! But what did you do to yourself?"

He had to admit that he was mesmerized by Esperanza's new look. The perfect makeup, nearly unnoticeable. The haircut, so sleek and citylike. He had to admit, too, that he still hadn't reached the limit of his love for her.

"Do you want to confess?"

He needed to know everything. What kind of trouble had she gotten into up north? He motioned Fidencio to leave them alone.

"At this point I am even more confused about what a sin is and what isn't. I'm sure I have much to confess, but I didn't come to do that." Esperanza turned off the TV, pulled up a chair, and sat in front of him. "I came to tell you that I found Blanca."

"Oh, Lord." Father Salvador missed the electric fan in his confessional box. He felt out of breath. How could Esperanza break such news in such a blunt way? One day she'd give him a heart attack.

"I found her early this week. I came home just to stand in front of my dirty stove and wait for my saint's orders, and all I found was an oven so clean my mother would have hugged me if she'd seen it. It was so squeaky clean that all I could see was the reflection of my own face. Soledad had left it spotless, Father. How could she dare? It's my oven. It's my grime!"

"I'm sure she didn't mean to cut your communication with San Judas Tadeo."

"But she did, Father. I yelled at her. I've never done that before. I was furious. I locked myself in the bathroom."

"Did she apologize?"

"Not only that. She promised she wouldn't question my beliefs anymore."

"That is a big step for her, Esperanza."

"I know. That's why I opened the bathroom door. We hugged and forgave each other. I was tired after the long trip and fighting with her stressed me out even more, so I told her I'd take a bath while she fixed dinner. My bathroom is large, just like the ones I'm sure you've been to in these old homes, with a big wall covered by tile on its lower half. I was just getting undressed when a power surge left me in the dark. Maybe San Judas Tadeo was behind it. So I lit some candles. I was there for a long time. My fingertips got all wrinkled from being in the water so long. Soledad came in the bathroom and sponged my back. I'm sure she felt guilty for what she'd done. Neither of us spoke. Then she put two towels on the chair by the bathtub and said, 'I'll go and set the table. Don't you get cold.' And that's when it all happened. As soon as she left, a smell of fresh-sliced papaya with lime juice floated all over the bathroom. My nose itched and a loud sneeze shot out of my nose. Then I heard a voice. It was the voice of Blanca. I heard it so clearly I thought she was standing there, right next to me. I looked in every direction. 'Mommy,' I heard again, but I couldn't see anything. Then I looked toward the wall, by the sink. There is a great rust stain from a leaky pipe dripping down next to the medicine cabinet and all the way to the tile. In that stain, I saw Blanca's face. She was wearing a beautiful Jarocha costume. She said, 'Mommy, you and me, we'll always be together.' Oh, Father Salvador, I'm so grateful to God I never got around to calling the plumber. She said, 'I'll always be here for you, Mommy.' "

"Oh, my Lord!"

"Father, do you understand? I finally know what San Judas Tadeo meant. Blanca is not dead. Blanca is not alive. She is in that little space in between. That's where I was supposed to look for her. If only I had let my saint finish his sentence, after 'Blanca is not dead . . . ,' I would have heard, 'Blanca is not alive.' Now I know where she is."

Never did Father Salvador imagine that Esperanza's search for Blanquita would end in a sanctification.

"So, what will you do now?" he asked, trying to be at least a little pragmatic. "Will you notify the Vatican?"

"Blanca's apparitions are not important to the rest of the world. Why do you think she's appearing before me on my bathroom wall and not before the whole town on the bridge wall moss, like San Juan Nepomuceno did six years ago? This is just between the two of us. She's my own little saint, my little *santita*. So, please don't start any paperwork."

"Heavens no! We can't even afford it. Do you have any idea of the costs involved in a beatification? Your relationship with your daughter will remain as private as you wish. You have my word."

"Thank you, Father. I won't tell anybody, either. Only you and Soledad. I've forbidden her to fix the leak. I told her, and she promised not to touch it."

"Now, I suggest you go to the cemetery."

"I already did, Father. But first I stopped by the hardware store and bought the brightest fuchsia paint they had. I arrived at Blanca's grave when the sun still dawdled below a thick dark cloud. Her resting place didn't look anything like I had seen it last. At first I didn't even recognize it. The loose soil is gone. Now it is covered with weeds. Wildflowers have sprung up all around the mausoleums. Have you been to the cemetery lately, Father? It gets so pretty this time of the year. You should go this weekend and have a picnic."

"But who do you want me to go with?" asked Father Salvador, hoping deeply it could be with Esperanza, but knowing it would not happen.

"Ask Doña Carmelita. She can cook something up for you. Something you really crave. When I was there, five children dressed as angels came with their mother to visit their grandparents and had a picnic. I saw them when I was pulling out some of the longest weeds around Blanca's tomb. They set a red tablecloth on their orchid purple gravestones and laid out all the food. They played hide-and-seek. One of the little girls got her wings stuck in a wrought-iron cross. The mother had to take them off. I would have helped her, but I was busy cleaning the crucifix on Blanca's tomb. It had the inscription 'In memory of Blanca Díaz.' The words 'In case' had been scratched out so that it read, 'she is here.' Soledad had ordered a large cement slab, two meters by one, to be built on top of the grave. There is a small glass case with Blanca's picture inside, along with a sophisticated brooch I had bought for her when she had her surgery. I touched the glass with the tips of my fingers and made the sign of the cross. When I had almost finished painting the slab, I discovered Soledad watching me from behind a gravestone."

"She followed you to the cemetery? I thought she wasn't going to interfere with your beliefs anymore."

"She isn't. But she doesn't want me to leave the house by myself. She says somebody might hurt me if I walk alone in the street. She says my thinking is not straight."

"Yes. I've heard people saying that you've lost your mind. That you couldn't take one more death in your family. This kind of gossip travels fast in this town."

"It bothers me. I know people are talking about me, rocking their rocking chairs in every other portico, sitting around tables in the coffee shop, but what can I do? I live here. I will have to live with this. As for Soledad, I don't know what to tell her. She wants me to stop talking to my saints. She hears me say things out loud to Blanca in the bathroom. She has been following me around. She's probably here, hiding somewhere, waiting for me to come out of church to guide me home. When I saw her at the cemetery, I called to her. She realized I had caught her. She was blushing. She came over and hugged me. I said to her, 'I really like what you did with Blanca's tomb. I love the glass case.' She said, 'Blanca would have loved that fuchsia you're painting her tomb with.' And I said, 'She does. She picked it out herself.'"

"What are you saying?" This was a true test of faith for Father Salvador.

"When I spoke with Blanca in the bathroom, I asked her what color she wanted me to paint her grave. She said, 'Fuchsia.' I'm sure Soledad is convinced I'm insane. We finished fixing the grave together. And that's what I came to tell you."

Father Salvador asked her to pray a rosary, not as penance, but as a way of thanking the Lord for allowing her such a miraculous encounter with her daughter.

Esperanza went to the pews. Father Salvador stayed in the sacristy.

"Dear God. My dearest God," he said aloud, but then continued in silence: I am so grateful to You for bringing Esperanza back. I will not let You down. I will stay away from her. I swear. I swear to You. She will not know how I feel about her. I will never tell her that I have imagined her in my bed, naked, her body spread over mine. She will come for confession and I will listen just as if she were any other parishioner. She will come to Mass. I will not look for her among the congregation. I'll run into her at the market. I'll greet her politely. I'll hear about her. I will answer with small talk. I will live in this town, breathing the same air that she breathes, bathing in the same river, eating fruit off the same trees, admiring the same landscape, watching and talking about the same soap operas, and ultimately being buried under the same soil. And that will be my cross. And I will carry it on my shoulders. And I will willingly be nailed to it until I die because You chose this test for me. But what I cannot do is change the way I feel. My love for her is an act as involuntary as my stomach's digestion. But I will keep my distance. Amen.

Father Salvador finished his prayer and continued his repair work purposely to show God that life went on and that everything was just as He expected. He replaced Santo Niño de Atocha's chair seat, swollen from humidity. The straw had split. Living in the tropics took its toll on the saints. More so on the ones made out of wood, for whom rot was destiny.

The church was quiet except for the squawking

noises of a pair of green parrots perched up on the chandelier. Esperanza was alone, kneeling in one of the pews. She prayed the rosary and between Hail Mary and Hail Mary, she thanked God. She thanked San Judas Tadeo. She thanked all her saints, one by one, until her prayer was interrupted by a voice whispering in her ear, "Let's go outside. I can't be wearing this in church."

Esperanza turned around to find El Angel Justiciero's mask-covered face two centimeters away from hers. She hadn't heard him come in. Maybe he'd just floated in. Maybe the noise of his steps had been covered up by the parrots' squawks. But how could she have missed his sweet smell? The camelias were responsible. They were blooming, and their scent had taken over the whole town. But there he was in person. El Angel Justiciero. He knelt right next to her, wearing his gala outfit.

They both made the sign of the cross quickly and walked out of the church. As they left, he enveloped her with his feathered cape, and right outside the entrance door, he kissed her for two entire minutes.

Father Salvador saw them from the altar. He picked up a vase with a wilted flower arrangement and walked back inside the sacristy. He felt like a body whose soul had been fiercely snatched. He had to sit. Why was that angel kissing Esperanza? Was he taking her away? Was God playing a bad joke on him? Why was there a sudden pain behind his ribs? He was not going to find an answer to those questions. As promised, he would watch Esperanza leave in the arms of that magnificent angel just as he would watch any other parishioner do the same.

*   *   *

"How did you find me?"

"It doesn't take a detective. There's only one Tlaco-talpan, Veracruz."

Esperanza and El Angel Justiciero sat on a quarry bench by the plaza's kiosk.

"But why did you come all the way down here?"

"Why did you leave without telling me? If you had told me you wanted to go back home, I would have brought you here in my truck. It's a lot faster than a bus. Haven't you understood I'm with you no matter what?"

They kissed, now for three minutes.

"Let's go back to L.A. We'll get married in Tijuana so you can enter the country legally," he said.

"I can't. I'm staying in Tlacotalpan."

"Esperanza, what's holding you here? Is it Soledad?"

"No, Angel. It's Blanca. I found her. She appears to me in a rust stain on my bathroom wall."

"She is a saint!"

"Can you believe it?"

"I do."

A little boy recognized El Angel Justiciero, no doubt from a wrestling magazine. He brought a paper napkin from the ice cream shop down the street and asked him for an autograph. His friends waited for him behind the kiosk. Angel signed the napkin and hugged the boy. He went to show the other children the signature, and they all ran off with the valued prize, giggling toward the dock.

"So, now that you've found your daughter, won't you come back to Los Angeles and marry me?"

"I'm sorry, Angel. I can't."

Angel drove his pickup truck. He headed north. He listened to norteña music in order to distract himself from his thoughts. He remembered wondering what would he do if he didn't find Esperanza. Suicide? That would be the last thing he'd ever do. Then the slightest hope of seeing her again would be buried with him. Besides, such a drastic solution wasn't in his personality. He was a fighter. He'd look for her tirelessly while she looked tirelessly for her daughter. But then, what if he found her and she didn't return to Los Angeles with him? The possibility had scared him like no opponent in the ring ever had. Life without Esperanza would be no life at all. He would just go back to Los Angeles alone and become a vegetable. He would change his name from El Angel Justiciero to the Flavorless Celery. His outfit would be pale green.

He drove past a gas station in the middle of the jungle that had a gigantic ice cream cone as an advertisement to attract travelers into the adjacent cafeteria. He remembered that right there on his way to Tlacotalpan, he had imagined Esperanza sleeping in his bed, immobile and peaceful. A child with no guilt.

"I've searched for you everywhere and I haven't found you, all I want is to be by your side," he sang out the window with all his strength to the rhythm of his

blasting stereo. "I'll move mountains, oceans, and val-
leys. I won't rest until I find you."

When he passed an old accident site marked by
twenty-six white wooden crosses, the thought of fate
came to his mind. He was amazed by the way God
reworks events so that people's paths gets more and
more entangled, and they end up having relationships
that seem at first as if they were not meant to be.

"It doesn't matter what fate has in store for us, I'll
love you till death do us part. I can handle the blows
of life, but if I lose you, it'll be a deep wound," he sang
even louder.

He drove by a roadside brothel. He knew Esperanza
had worked as a prostitute, but he also knew she wasn't
one. It didn't take a detective to know that. She said she
still had to sort out exactly what she had learned from
her experience. The only thing she was certain of was
that she would never have walked up to El Angel Justiciero that night at the arena if she hadn't met those
other men first.

So he sang, "I don't care what's in your past, to me
your soul is spotless, I'll forgive you, rain or thunder,
because with me, it's starting anew. I'll do the impossible, even what can't be done, because hope is the last to
die . . . yeah . . . yeah. Hope is the last to die."

He sang so loud that he woke Esperanza up. She
rubbed her eyes and put her hand on his lap. She had
slept through two entire states and had missed the
impressive transformation of the landscape from jungle
to desert.

"I painted the house colonial blue with Indian red around the doors and windows," he said.

"That's funny. I was just dreaming about the house."

"Don't tell me you want to change the color."

"No. Blue is fine outside. I was dreaming that we were painting the children's room California poppy orange."

He stretched his seat belt to kiss her neck.

"I still can't believe you showed up in church wearing your Angel Justiciero costume."

"Outfit, please," he corrected her gently. "I figured maybe it would be easier to talk you into coming back with me to Los Angeles that way."

They passed a sign that read: UNITED STATES BORDER 200 KILOMETERS. Esperanza's box of saints was in the back of the truck along with a couple of suitcases. Next to them, tightly fastened with ropes, was an entire wall from Esperanza's bathroom, complete with tile, sink, medicine cabinet, light fixture, toilet, pipes, and the rust stain.

"We should have built another bathroom for Soledad before leaving," said Esperanza. "We shouldn't have left her in the lurch."

"She'll be fine. She can use a bucket for a while."

"I hope her beloved mariachi knows about masonry and plumbing."

"He can't afford to get blisters on his fingers."

"If not him, someone else will help her build it. Did you notice the two veiled ladies in front of church? They saw us leave. They're better than any local newspaper.

They'll make sure the whole town knows we took the bathroom. I can imagine them on their porches twenty-five years from now, rocking their chairs, still gossiping about us and the cargo we hauled away."

Esperanza smiled comfortably. They wouldn't understand. She looked out the window. Rolling tumbleweeds barely scratched the smooth desert sand, leaving streams of incomprehensible hieroglyphs along their path, soon to be erased by the wind of the barren Sonora. She cuddled on Angel's shoulder and went back to her dream.

A SCRIBNER PAPERBACK FICTION
READING GROUP GUIDE

ESPERANZA'S BOX OF SAINTS

Esperanza's Box of Saints is a magical, humorous, and passion-filled odyssey about a beautiful young widow's search for her missing child—a mission that takes her from a humble Mexican village to the rowdy brothels of Tijuana and a rarely seen side of Los Angeles. But it's not just a geographical journey—it's also a journey of self-discovery.

DISCUSSION QUESTIONS

1. What did you think of Esperanza's apparitions? Are they serious? Comical? Rooted in religion? Why do you think the author chose San Judas Tadeo to be her patron saint?

2. Esperanza carries her box of saints wherever she goes. What do you think this box represents? Is it the mobility of faith? Or perhaps the saints are protection from evil? Why do you think strangers find her altar so intriguing?

3. Are you convinced that Blanca really died in the hospital, or do you believe that she's still alive? Did your opinion change at different times during the book? If so, when? Did you agree with Esperanza's intuition?

4. Esperanza has been living with Soledad for twelve years. Do you think their relationship is supportive or destructive? What does Soledad's presence bring to the plot and to Esperanza's mental and physical well-being?

5. How do you think Esperanza's major losses (husband and only child) at such a young age have affected her and her outlook on life?

6. What role do shoes play in Esperanza's journey? She's always searching for the perfect shoes—then ruining or losing them. What do you think this says about her?

7. When Esperanza goes from brothel to brothel while searching for Blanca, she meets some interesting characters along the way. Do you think it's realistic that each one breaks the rules for Esperanza? What is it about her innocence that allows her to remain unharmed?

8. The bulk of the novel takes place in Southern California and Mexico. Did the pace and spirit of the writing give you a tangi-

ble sense of place and cultural background? How did Esperanza's surroundings affect the plot?

9. Did you ever think that Esperanza would find love and trust in another adult? Did you expect someone like Angel to be her savior? How did you think the tale would end?

10. On the surface, Esperanza dramatically reinvents herself to survive, but after she completes her odyssey—and her journey of self-discovery—do you think she's still the same person inside?

BIOGRAPHY

Born in Mexico, MARÍA AMPARO ESCANDÓN now lives in Los Angeles where she cofounded a Spanish-language advertising agency with her husband. She teaches writing through the UCLA Extension service, and her stories have been published in many magazines.

WHY I WROTE *Esperanza's Box of Saints* BY MARÍA AMPARO ESCANDÓN

Esperanza's Box of Saints became a novel after a question popped up in my mind: What if I was told that my daughter had died and I wasn't able to confirm her death? My immediate answer would be to deny it. To prove them wrong I would do what anyone else would in this case: anything and everything. Call on otherworldly forces for guidance? Sure. Set out to find her who knows where in the world? Of course. Become a prostitute? You bet. And in the process of looking for her, I'd most likely find myself. And so Esperanza embarks on this magical, amusing yet enlightening, serious yet irreverent journey of self-discovery. I wanted to write a painful comedy in a quirky, whimsical, bold, sensuous, agile way that could make the reader laugh to tears in the midst of the tragedy. I also wanted to keep this story outside the margins of magic realism. Why keep magic within the parameters of extraordinary worlds when it abounds in real life? Esperanza's story is magical reality, the kind that people who live in Mexico encounter every day.

To learn more about *Esperanza's Box of Saints* and to correspond with the author, visit María Amparo Escandón on the World Wide Web at:

http://www.esperanzasboxofsaints.com